HIDDEN GIFTS

A Castle Mountain Lodge Romance

ELENA AITKEN

Ink Blot Communications

Also by Elena Aitken

Castle Mountain Lodge

Unexpected Gifts

Hidden Gifts

Unexpected Endings - Short Story

Mistaken Gifts

Secret Gifts

Goodbye Gifts

Tempting Gifts

Holiday Gifts

Promised Gifts

Accidental Gifts

The Castle Mountain Lodge Collection: Books 1-3

The Castle Mountain Lodge Collection: Books 4-6

The Castle Mountain Lodge Collection: Books 7-9

The Castle Mountain Lodge Complete Collection

The Springs Series

Summer of Change

Falling Into Forever

Second Glances

Winter's Burn

Midnight Springs

She's Making A List

Summit of Desire

Summit of Seduction

Summit of Passion

Fighting For Forever

The Springs Collection: Volume 1

The Springs Collection: Volume 2

The Springs Collection: Volume 3

The Springs Complete Collection - Books 1-10

Destination Paradise

Shelter by the Sea

Escape to the Sun

Hidden in the Sand

Ever After

Choosing Happily Ever After

Needing Happily Ever After

Wanting Happily Ever After

Fighting Happily Ever After

We Wish You A Happily Ever After

Keeping Happily Ever After

Finding Happily Ever After

Seeking Happily Ever After

Cherishing Happily Ever After

Ever After: Volume One (Books 1-4)

The McCormicks

Love in the Moment

His to Defend

His to Tame

His to Seek

Hers for the Season

Bears of Grizzly Ridge: Books 1-4

Bears of Grizzly Ridge: Books 5-8

Halfway Series

Halfway to Nowhere

Halfway in Between

Halfway to Christmas

Chapter One

CASTLE MOUNTAIN LODGE was just gearing up for the busy summer season with only a few people milling around the lobby. As far as Bo Clancy was concerned, it was perfect. The last thing he needed to worry about was an audience on top of everything else. He paced in front of the fireplace and glanced around again for the staff manager. He'd been told that Carmen would be in the lobby, but so far he hadn't seen her. It figured that just when he needed to talk to her, she would be busy. They still had a few weeks before the summer season was in full swing, which was good since it bought him a little more time to figure out what he was going to do.

Bo had been set up to have another successful summer as the lead outdoor guide at Castle Mountain. He'd been running the summer program at the Lodge for the past three years and it was the perfect job for someone like him. Someone who'd rather be outside than in and, most important, didn't have any family ties that would keep him from leading the overnight excursions. They were the most lucrative trips because of the tips involved, usually from the women. He'd gained a bit of a reputation as a flatterer and as a result was often specially requested to lead ladies' groups. He never acted on his flirtations, at least not with the guests, but it didn't hurt as far as the income was concerned.

That was all going to change this year, unless he could figure things out. Bo looked at the couch, where Ella was sound asleep. Curled up with his big cable-knit sweater as a blanket, she looked impossibly small. Her blond hair was fanned over her tiny arm that was tucked under her head. Her blond eyelashes fluttered against her porcelain cheeks. Bo stopped pacing and stood transfixed by her every breath. It didn't matter how many times he looked at the birth certificate and read the letter, he still couldn't believe she was his. He bent to touch her, to push the stray hair off her cheek, but he pulled away at the last minute, a familiar voice intruding on the moment.

Bo straightened up to see Carmen, accompanied by two other women, walking across the room. They stopped by the grand piano and he watched for a minute as Carmen gestured around the grand foyer. She seemed familiar with the petite, dark-haired woman—maybe they were frequent guests? But no, the other woman, the taller one, clutched a red binder in her hands. The Castle Mountain Lodge Employee Manual. He had one just like it somewhere in his bags. Not that he'd ever looked at it.

Carmen had never been his biggest fan. Not since the first year they'd worked together and he'd slept with her roommate. He was fairly certain the roommate didn't remember it—it had been years ago—but Carmen had been frosty to him ever since. When he'd discovered that she was now in charge of staff, he'd been dreading the conversation he needed to have because based on past history, she wasn't likely to help him out.

Bo took another look at Ella, still sleeping on the couch. "No time like the present," he said aloud. He turned and crossed the room in three long strides. "Excuse me," he said, interrupting the women. "Carmen, I need to speak with you."

Carmen turned, a fake smile that didn't quite reach her eyes pasted on her face. "Nice to see you, Bo. I'm just in the middle of something right now. Maybe we can catch up later."

"It can't wait," he said. He flicked his glance to the other women and his gaze naturally landed on the taller of the two. She looked to be in her late twenties, which instantly intrigued him. Older than most of the women working at the Lodge and she was attractive, very attractive. But she definitely had the look of a city girl who wouldn't know the first thing about stepping out of the mall and onto the trail. Despite her slender waist and curves that begged to have his hands on them, city girls weren't his thing. Even if he were looking for a diversion, which he wasn't. "I am sorry to interrupt, darling," he spoke to her and turned on the charm. "You probably have a lot of questions about the Lodge and the mountains, after all, they can be intimidating. And I'm sure we can do our best to answer those for you later." Without waiting for a response, he turned back to Carmen. "I do need to speak to you right now."

Carmen cleared her throat and stood tall. "Bo, this is Andi Williams and Morgan Pierce." She waved at the two women in turn. "Andi is a good friend of the Lodge and Morgan will be working with us this summer."

He spared a quick nod but kept his eyes on Carmen. "Hi," he said in the women's direction. "Carmen—"

"Oh, I'm sure a big important guy like yourself can answer all the questions for little ol' me," the voice interrupted him, and Bo turned back to the attractive woman, batting her eyelashes in jest. "And maybe when you're finished," she drawled, "you could protect me from all the big bad bears in the scary dark woods?"

Amused, and more than a little intrigued, Bo tilted his head and examined the woman for a moment. She batted her lashes one more time before her eyes hardened and challenged him. He'd underestimated her.

Next to her, the other woman stifled a laugh that Bo ignored. "I certainly didn't mean to imply that you were incapable of taking care of yourself," he said, a sly grin on his face.

"Of course not."

The two faced off, neither willing to break the stare. For a moment Bo even forgot what he'd come to talk to Carmen about but before he had a chance to say anything further, Carmen reminded him of his purpose.

"Bo, if you could just give me five minutes to finish up—"

"No," the woman said. Damn, he wished he'd been paying attention when Carmen introduced them. "It seems that—Bo, is it?" She waited for his nod before continuing, "It seems that Bo here has something very pressing to talk to you about. I'm sure Andi can help me get settled." She ran a hand through her hair; a nervous action that contrasted completely with her no-nonsense attitude and Bo had to hide a smile.

Despite his vow to focus on Ella, he couldn't ignore the familiar tug low in his belly.

"You're sure, Morgan?" Carmen asked.

Morgan, Bo remembered. He made a mental note of the name; he wouldn't forget it again.

She smiled at Carmen. All the challenge and hardness that Morgan had shown him a moment ago was gone, replaced by a warmth that he suddenly wished was aimed in his direction. "It's no problem, really," she said. "Besides, Andi has been dying to show me some of her favorite spots."

"It's true," Andi said. "And it'll give me a chance to enjoy the Lodge in the spring. Don't worry, Carmen. We can see that you're busy."

"Thank you both for being so understanding," Carmen said, shooting a dirty look in Bo's direction. She handed Morgan a piece of paper. "This is your room assignment. Your roommate should be there soon, if she's not already. There's just one more thing that I need to discuss with you. There's been a little change in your job assignment, but...you know what? I'll find you later to talk it over. Is that okay?"

"Sure."

"It was a pleasure to meet you, Morgan," Bo said in his most charming voice. "I'm sure I'll be seeing you again."

"I guess we'll see," Morgan said. Her arms were crossed over her chest, but Bo noticed the spark in her eye when she spoke. Was it a challenge? She looked as if she might say something else, but her friend took her arm and led her away. It was probably for the better. He needed to focus on Ella and a woman like that would only be an unwelcome distraction.

The moment they were out of earshot, Carmen spun on her heel to face him. "Bo, what the hell is wrong with you?"

"It's good to see you, too, Carmen." His forced smile faded. "Congrats on your promotion, by the way."

"Stop it." Her mouth was a hard line. "I see you still think your charm and good looks can get you whatever you want. But as you already know, it doesn't work on me." She tightened her grip on her clipboard.

"You think I'm good-looking?"

Contempt shot out of her eyes and he quickly readjusted his approach. Bo leaned his elbows on the shiny piano top. He was pretty sure that charm wouldn't be enough to smooth things over with her; clearly, he'd been right.

"I did get a promotion," she said, ignoring him, "thank you. And I have a lot to do, so what's so important?"

"You know I'm looking forward to another busy summer up here," he started. "I always accept this position over any others that are offered."

"And others are offered?" she asked with a wry smile.

"You know they are."

"Okay." Carmen crossed her arms over her clipboard. "I'll admit it. You're the best, but why do I feel like you need something? I can't give you a raise, Bo. You already get paid more—"

"I don't need a raise." He spoke quickly and glanced over his shoulder to the couch. "But I do need a favor." Bo turned back to Carmen, who was frowning at him. "My circumstances have changed recently and I don't think staff housing is going to be acceptable."

"Pardon me?" Carmen swallowed a bitter laugh. "Shall we give you a suite then?"

"That would be great."

"I was kidding," Carmen said dryly, her laughter cut off.

Bo looked around the near-empty lobby and made a decision. He couldn't hope to keep Ella a secret forever, and Carmen was his best hope—his only hope really— to make the situation more comfortable. "Okay," he said. "Come here." He grabbed Carmen's arm and led her to the couch, where Ella was still asleep.

"Who's this?"

"My daughter." He said the word aloud for the first time. It felt foreign, but not entirely unpleasant, on his tongue.

Carmen's face clouded with confusion. "But she's at least—"

"Four. She's four."

"I had no idea…"

"Neither did I." Bo gestured to an empty sofa.

When they were settled where he could still keep an eye on Ella, Bo said, "You can see my predicament?"

"I can see it," she said. "But I don't understand it."

Bo sighed. He couldn't avoid the truth. "Ella's mother just

died. It was breast cancer and it apparently moved quite quickly."

"That's terrible," Carmen said.

"It is." Bo nodded. "I knew Tessa years ago when we were in college. I had no idea she was sick. Heck, I had no idea she was pregnant." His gaze drifted back to the sleeping child as he thought of Tessa and how difficult it must have been for her to have a child on her own. They'd both been young and stupid. Obviously, too stupid.

"You mean, you didn't know?"

Bo shook his head.

"Then? How?"

"I got a call from Social Services a few days ago. They told me Tessa had died about a month ago and left a child behind. Like I said, I had no idea that she existed, but apparently Tessa had laid it out quite clearly in a letter that she wanted Ella to live with me, her father. It took them a while to find me, I was—"

"I don't understand."

"Oh, trust me, neither do I." Bo ran a hand through his hair and looked Carmen squarely in the eyes. "Look. I know this is unusual, but I really would appreciate some help here while I'm figuring things out. I mean, obviously she can't stay with me."

Carmen raised an eyebrow.

"No," Bo said. "She's not staying with me. Well, I mean, she is. At least for a little bit, but I'm going to do some searching into Tessa's family. There has to be a better place for her to live than—" Bo stopped talking abruptly. Why was he telling her all this? He looked at Ella's tiny body, her chest rising and falling with every soft breath. He ignored the pull in his chest and turned back to Carmen. "Anyway, I need a little help. Just until I can figure things out. Ella's going through a tough enough time. She doesn't need the drama of living in staff housing."

"You're right," Carmen said. "It's no place for a child. But there's really nowhere else."

It was a long shot, but he voiced his idea anyway. "I know you were kidding but, what about a suite?"

Carmen half coughed, half laughed and quickly covered her mouth in an effort to quiet herself. After a moment, she regained control and said to Bo, "A suite? Please tell me you're kidding."

Bo didn't answer. Instead, he waited her out, his gaze fixed on Carmen's face.

"Bo?" Carmen blinked hard and wiped her eyes. "You know I can't give you a suite. What about the other staff? The guests? The cost?" She flipped open her clipboard and started looking through the pages. "There must be an empty room available in staff quarters…"

He still didn't say anything. Carmen looked up. "I can't give you a suite," she said again. "Really, you shouldn't even have a child here. This isn't a—"

"Look." His voice was low, barely contained. "I don't need to hear how you think I should or should not have Ella here. The fact is, she is here. Now can you help me out or do I need to find a new job for the summer?"

Carmen tucked her clipboard under her crossed arms and matched Bo's glare. "You wouldn't leave."

"Try me."

Tension sparked around them as they continued their stare down. Bo hadn't planned to threaten her with quitting. The fact was he couldn't afford to quit. He needed his situation at Castle Mountain to work out. But Carmen didn't know that. And he was counting on her not calling his bluff.

A tiny noise, almost a squeak, came from the couch. The sound broke Bo's heart, and the standoff with Carmen.

In two quick steps, he was kneeling on the floor next to Ella. Hair mussed from her nap, her brown eyes were still clouded with sleep, but were open wide taking in the big room. He reached out and tentatively tucked a stray hair behind her ear. He moved to hug her, or hold her hand or maybe just touch her again, but he pulled away. Bo'd never been comfortable around children, and that hadn't changed in the last few days. The little girl didn't seem to be any more comfortable with him, either, and she pulled her legs up to her chest and hugged herself into a ball.

"Did you have a good sleep?" he asked.

She nodded and jammed her thumb in her mouth.

"Soon we can get settled in our room and then you can have a real nap, okay?"

She nodded again.

Ella had said only a handful of words since he'd picked her up. And the Social Services woman said she would only speak to the foster mother she'd been placed with, but even then, she didn't say much. Not that Bo knew much about children, but he thought for four, she should be talking a lot more. Of course, maybe losing your mother and living with a foster family before being handed over to a total stranger was enough to make a little girl clam up.

"Are you hungry? Do you want a snack or something?"

Ella shook her head and turned to look out the window.

With a deep sigh, Bo pushed up on his thighs and stood. Carmen was looking at him in that way that women have, when they've been affected by a small child or a puppy. The way that meant she was going to help.

"So, I can have the suite," he said. It wasn't a question.

Carmen nodded. "I'll see what I can do. But it will only be for a few weeks until the busy season starts. And I'm going to have to charge you something for it."

"Take it out of my check."

She nodded and her expression turned to a frown. "Bo?" Carmen grabbed his arm and led him a few steps away from Ella. "Have you thought about what you're going to do with her while you're working? I mean, surely you don't plan to take her on hikes with you. She's so tiny."

"I was hoping she could go to the child- care room."

"Castle Cub's Club?"

Bo shrugged. "Is that what it's called?" He smiled to himself. He'd never given the Lodge's child-care program any thought. He'd never had to. "It's cute," he said and then quickly added, "I told you. It's just for a little bit. I need to make some calls. I think she has some family out East."

Carmen raised an eyebrow in his direction. But when she turned to look at Ella, she smiled and nodded her head. "Fine," she said. "I'll clear it with the powers that be."

"Thank you." Bo breathed a deep sigh of relief.

"This isn't a permanent solution." Carmen's voice permeated his thoughts.

"Don't I know it," Bo said with a vague nod. He partly listened as Carmen continued to speak about getting a room key. But his focus had already shifted squarely back to the little girl sitting on the couch. She looked so lost, so scared, and so alone. At least they had that in common.

Chapter Two

MORGAN'S BEDROOM WAS TINY. It had just enough room for a single bed and a dresser. Fortunately, the view out the window made up for whatever charm the room lacked. It didn't matter how many times she looked around, she couldn't get over the raw beauty of her new home. At least the outside of it.

She tossed one of her duffles onto the mattress and moved back out to the living room of the small staff residence apartment she'd be sharing with the roommate she hadn't met yet. Morgan would have preferred to get her own apartment, but apparently that wasn't an option as the Lodge had a lot of employees and not enough accommodations. She wasn't happy about it, but she'd make the best of it. Besides, it might be good for her to get to know someone. If she were determined to make her new life work out, she'd need some new friends.

Andi was one of her best friends, but she couldn't understand why Morgan was dead set on leaving. Before she'd left, they'd had what was becoming a very familiar conversation.

"I don't get it," Andi said. She'd been lounging on

Morgan's bed, watching her unpack. "You know I love it here, but living here?"

"Why not?" Morgan hung another shirt and turned to her friend. "I've been listening to you go on and on about this place for so long—what better place to get a fresh start?"

"That's just it, Morgan. Why a fresh start? You're a child psychologist. I don't understand why you'd give up a great job to—"

"I told you," Morgan turned away again, "I can't work with kids anymore."

"That was only the opinion of one doctor, Morgan. You'll have—"

"I don't want to talk about it."

And she didn't. Nothing Andi could say would take away the sting of the doctor's news. She'd tried to push past the diagnosis, and for a while she went to work as if nothing had changed. But every day it got harder and finally she put in her notice, giving up the career she'd worked so hard for.

"It's time for a change," Morgan said more to herself than to her friend. "This will be good."

"It will be good." Silently, Andi got up from the bed and slid her arm around Morgan, giving her a squeeze. "You're going to love it here. After all, it is kind of a magical place."

Morgan turned to face her and laughed. "Just because you met Colin here doesn't mean everyone finds their Prince Charming in the mountains. Besides that, I'm not interested."

"You say that now."

"And always. Now help me unpack or get out of here."

Together, they unpacked all of Morgan's things and then she did leave. As nice as it had been to have Andi introduce her to Carmen, and help her get a job planning events at the Lodge, it was nice to have her friend leave so she could get settled.

Alone, Morgan looked around her new accommodations. It

was definitely small, but it was cute. And a blank slate. There weren't really any decorations to speak of, not that she had any. But maybe her mysterious roommate would have a flair for decorating?

Morgan wandered over to the patio door and slid it open, letting a rush of crisp mountain air inside. She'd been hoping to ask Carmen about who her roommate might be, or even when she'd be arriving. But they'd been interrupted before she could ask her question. Interrupted by a very handsome man, she thought with a smile. She wrapped her sweater tightly around her and stepped out onto the balcony. He may have been nice to look at, but he'd been a total jerk, interrupting them the way he had. Who does that? Morgan shook her head, trying to get the man out of her thoughts. The last thing she needed was a man, even one that good-looking, in her life.

Morgan peered over the edge of the balcony, letting the cool air clear her thoughts. Three large staff residence buildings circled around an open green field that held some picnic tables and a large fire pit. The buildings reminded Morgan of rustic dorms, especially as there were people coming and going, carrying boxes and bags. At least she wouldn't be the only newbie.

"You're going to freeze to death out there."

Morgan turned to see the source of the voice. A tall, extremely thin woman stood behind her in the doorway. She was wearing what looked like a fisherman's sweater over a long skirt and tights; a bandanna on her head held back dozens of long, tiny braids; and a gold hoop in her nose sparkled in the sunlight. Morgan tried not to stare, but she'd never seen anyone quite like the woman who stood in front of her.

"My name is Astrid," the woman said. She extended one long thin arm, bracelets and bangles jingling with the movement.

Morgan took her hand and shook it. "Morgan," she said. "You must be my roommate."

"The one and only," Astrid said with a smile. Her green eyes sparkled and she did a quick spin on the balcony, stopping with her arms raised to the sky. Her sweater slid down, revealing bare skin, adorned with intricate brown lines and swirls. "We're going to have a brilliant summer," she said, and in that moment, Morgan decided that maybe having a roommate wouldn't be so bad after all. It might, in fact, be quite interesting.

"So you're going to be in event planning?" Astrid asked. Morgan was sitting on their brown couch, sipping a mug of tea, watching her new roommate buzz around their living room.

"I am. I've worked with my friend in her business a little bit, so I have some experience, but I didn't go to school for it or anything."

"School?" Astrid stopped, a bright purple cloth dangling from her fingertips. "Like college?"

Morgan nodded.

"That's cool," Astrid said. "I find the idea of higher education oppressing. But I get that for some people, they need the accomplishment of finishing a program."

For a moment, Morgan thought she should be insulted, but she wasn't. In the last few hours, she'd come to see that Astrid spoke her mind, without much regard for what other people might be thinking. She wasn't a malicious or mean person, just straightforward, and Morgan liked it.

"Why am I not surprised?"

Astrid laughed. "I know it's kinda cliché, but I can't help it. I just don't get the whole school thing."

Morgan shrugged. There was a lot about Astrid that was

cliché. But the fact that she didn't seem to care is what made her so unique.

"So if you didn't go to school for parties," Astrid continued, "what did you go to school for? Because you do look like the type that went." She laughed and again, instead of being insulted the way she thought she should be, Morgan laughed along with her.

"I have a degree in child development."

Astrid stopped and stared at her. "Child development? As in, how children develop?"

"That's the kind."

"So you're here because…"

"Because the last thing I want to do is work with children."

Astrid narrowed her eyes in question but Morgan only offered her sweetest smile as way of explanation.

"Makes perfect sense to me," Astrid said. She turned and grabbed something that might have been a vase out of a box.

It was actually kind of refreshing to be honest with someone about her career choice. At least, partly honest, anyway. But the way Morgan justified it, it wasn't her fault Astrid didn't ask her why she didn't want to work with kids. So as long as she didn't ask, Morgan didn't need to tell and that's the way she preferred it.

"So where do you work?" Morgan asked, happy to shift the focus off her. She was enjoying sitting back and letting Astrid decorate their space. The decor was shaping up to be a really unique mixture of hippy and outdoorsy with a bit of modern convenience thrown in.

"I'm in housekeeping," Astrid said. "I know it's not glamorous and front line and all that, but I really like it. You can learn a lot about people from their rooms."

"And you want to learn about the guests?"

"Sure I do," Astrid said. "It's only by learning about others that we learn about ourselves."

Morgan put down her tea and picked up a picture frame Astrid had placed on the table. Dozens of tiny pebbles were glued to the edge, making it quite heavy, but there was no picture inside.

Morgan pointed to where a picture should be and Astrid said, "It's bad karma to surround yourself with old memories."

Morgan raised her eyebrow, looked at the frame once more and put it back on the table. "I like that theory."

"You have some old memories you'd rather not be surrounded by," Astrid said. It wasn't a question.

The image of Justin, her last boyfriend, flashed in Morgan's mind, but she immediately pushed the thought of him away. It'd been six months since they'd broken up, but still Morgan couldn't help but think that things might be different if only she'd been different.

She shook her head and focused on her roommate as Astrid asked, "How do you feel about candles?"

"I don't know if I've ever had an opinion one way or the other about candles."

Astrid stood in the middle of the room with two large waxy pillars in her hands. "Really? You strike me as the romantic type. You don't have a boyfriend?"

"I need a boyfriend to enjoy candles?"

"That's not what I said." Astrid positioned the candles on a large cabinet that held a small television. "You just seem like the type of girl that has a boyfriend. You don't have one?" She moved back to a large shopping bag, pulling out a selection of pinecones in a variety of shapes and sizes.

"I don't," Morgan said. "Have a boyfriend, I mean." She watched while Astrid arranged the pinecones around the candles. The display was simple, but surprisingly beautiful. "That's nice."

Astrid turned around, a smile on her face. "That you don't have a boyfriend?"

"No. Well, yes." Morgan felt her face heat up. She jumped off the couch and moved to the shopping bag. "I meant the pinecones and you know it. What else do you have in here?" She dug through the bag and produced a clay sculpture of a moose—or maybe it was an owl—a few more candles, a large silk cloth that Astrid grabbed from her hand and draped over the couch, and a glass bowl. "You have a very interesting style," she said to Astrid.

"You like it?" She asked the question, but it was obvious Astrid wouldn't care either way.

"I do," Morgan said. "It's perfect. Where did you get it all?"

"Here and there," she said. "Some I picked up on my own, but most of these things were gifts."

"Gifts?" Morgan picked up the clay figure again. "Really?"

"You'd be surprised," Astrid said with a small smile. "If you're open and accepting of them, there are hidden gifts all over the place. When you least expect it, the universe will be very giving." Astrid took the figure out of Morgan's hands and stroked it lovingly. "Stay open, my friend, and ready to receive."

Morgan barely had time to let her words sink in before Astrid turned with a flourish. "Anyway, there're more candles, for when you have a boyfriend." She winked and Morgan tried not to groan. She'd been hoping that getting away from the city and her friends would get her away from the constant pressure to have a boyfriend, get married, and have kids. She didn't want that. Not anymore.

"Not to worry." Morgan tried to sound firm. "There will be no boys."

Astrid let out a sharp laugh and threw her head back. "Oh, sweetie. Why do you think I come back here every summer? There's nothing but men in the mountains. And what's more," she said, "you're going to meet some tonight."

"I didn't take you for the boy-crazy type," Morgan said. "And anyway, what's tonight?"

"Boy-crazy?" Astrid snorted. "Hardly. But I do like to be entertained. And what better way?" She winked and started tidying up what was left of her decorations. "Tonight is the start of that entertainment. The night before summer season, there's a welcome barbecue and bonfire in the common."

Morgan looked to where her roommate was pointing, out the window to the large grassy field that their balcony faced. "Sounds good," she said. And to her surprise, found that she meant it. Besides the fact that Morgan had no interest in men or the type of entertainment that Astrid was looking for, she had to admit it would be fun to get out and meet some new people. "What time?"

Chapter Three

BO WATCHED Ella wander around the hotel room that would be her bedroom. There should be toys. A little girl should have dolls and stuffed animals, not the elegant furnishings of a hotel suite. Even with his limited experience with children, he knew that.

"I know it's not very fun," he said. "Maybe we can get you some toys?" Ella turned and looked at him impassively. She blinked twice, her dark eyes giving nothing away. She turned and picked up the clay deer that adorned the dresser. "Maybe you shouldn't—"

He was going to tell her to put it down, that she shouldn't play with the decorations, but as he watched, Ella stroked the back of the little sculpture and looked up at him with her wide, innocent eyes. She popped her thumb in her mouth and looked at him expectantly.

"Never mind," he said. It wouldn't hurt if she played with it. After all, the poor kid didn't have anything else. "I'm going to be in the kitchen if you need anything, okay?"

He waited for Ella to respond, which she didn't. After a

moment, Bo let out a deep sigh and made his way down the hall.

In the kitchen, he poured himself a glass of water and leaned against the breakfast bar. He ran his hands through his hair and for at least the hundredth time that day, tried to figure out what he was going to do about the little girl in the other room.

He barely even remembered her mother Tessa. What they'd had together could hardly be classified as a relationship, which is probably why she hadn't bothered to contact him when she found out she was pregnant. Which is why it didn't make any sense that she would leave her daughter in his care, even for a little while. And it would only be a little while. There was no way he could be a father.

Bo's thoughts flew to the conversation he'd had with Clara Kersey, the woman from Social Services, only a few days earlier. They'd been standing in the lobby of the Best Western hotel. A small grey suitcase stood next to her, a little blond girl on her other side.

"It took us quite a while to find you, Mr. Clancy," Clara had said. "But I'm glad we did. Tessa wanted Ella to know her father. It's all in the letter."

Bo looked down to the little girl who had yet to look at him and back to Clara. "You've read the letter?"

"I have."

"And she wanted me to take Ella?" Bo asked. His brain swirled. He couldn't wrap his head around what was happening. "I don't know anything about children. I can't be a father."

"Turns out you already are." The woman's voice was brusque. "Look," she said, this time a little softer, "I know this must be a shock. But when there is a clear order of whom the child is to live with and that person checks out as you have, we're very inclined to follow that directive."

"But, I—"

"You are the biological father," Clara said.

"Surely she must have family?" Bo raked his hand through his thick dark hair. "Grandparents— an aunt or uncle? Someone."

"She does have an uncle on the East Coast. We've been in contact with him. He hadn't seen Tessa in years and he didn't even know about the child." Clara shifted so she was facing slightly away from Ella, who stood unmoved. She lowered her voice and said, "Look, Mr. Clancy, I'm sure you weren't really expecting to wake up this morning and be a dad, but it is the situation. We are extremely overworked with children who are in much more precarious situations. And you are the biological father."

Bo shook his head slowly but stopped when he saw the little girl staring at him with dark eyes so much like his own. "Where are her things?" he asked Clara, without taking his gaze off the child.

"This is it." The woman gestured to the suitcase and efficiently flipped open her clipboard. "I'll need you to sign here, Mr. Clancy."

Blindly, Bo signed the paper. In no time, Clara was gone and it was just Bo, alone with his daughter.

Looking back, it seemed as if it'd happened weeks ago, or even months. But it'd only been forty-eight hours. And Bo couldn't even begin to think about how he was going to survive another forty-eight. But there didn't seem to be a choice. The Social Services lady had more or less told him there was no where else for Ella to go. He stared down the empty hallway towards her room. Would it be better for her to go into the system, he wondered. He didn't know whether he could answer that honestly. Not yet.

"Ella," he called gently.

After a moment, the girl appeared in the doorway of her room, but made no move to walk towards him. He wasn't surprised when she didn't say anything. So far, Ella had only uttered a few words to him. So obviously the child could talk—she just refused to. Bo had no idea whether it was normal or not, but either way, he was getting used to her silence.

"Are you hungry?"

She nodded.

"Well, I think I know about a barbecue going on," he said and held out his hand to her. "Do you like hot dogs?"

Ella nodded and walked down the hall to meet him. To his surprise, she took his hand. It felt tiny and fragile in his large one, but he cupped it carefully.

"Okay, then," he said, "let's go get you some dinner." Bo looked down into her big, empty dark eyes. Her silence he could get used to, but the haunted, sad way she looked at him —that was much harder to take.

Bo tried to suppress a laugh as he watched Ella devour her second hot dog. For such a small girl, she had an impressive appetite. They were sitting in a relatively quiet patch of the lawn in the common area. Ella held the remains of a bun in one hand, the clay deer from the hotel suite in the other. He didn't think Carmen would be very happy about them absconding with it, but no matter how Carmen felt about him, Bo was pretty sure she wouldn't deny a little girl some semblance of a toy. Besides, if it were really a big deal, she could deduct it from his check. Bo tried not to think about his ever decreasing paycheck. The suite wasn't going to be cheap, even with the deal Carmen gave him, but he didn't have a lot of other choices. He was dead set against exposing Ella to the debauchery that could go down in staff housing. For that matter, it went against his better judgment to even bring her to the barbecue, but he'd hoped that if they arrived early enough he wouldn't have to subject Ella to much of the craziness that usually occurred at staff parties. He wouldn't have brought her at all if she hadn't needed to eat. As messed up as it was, he was trying to be a good dad, or guardian, or whatever he was.

"Are you full?" he asked her. "Because I could probably wrestle that guy for his hot dog." He pointed across the grass to a large muscled man who looked as if he was wearing a t-shirt two sizes too small. Ella stared at the man, her mouth hanging open. She shook her head from side to side so vehemently that her hair whipped around her face.

"Don't worry," Bo said with a chuckle. "That's Jeff. I work with him. He may look like a gorilla, but he's a total pushover." An idea popped into Bo's head. "Jeff works with the horses. Do you like horses?"

Ella's face split into a huge smile and she nodded. Bo couldn't help but notice that the smile didn't reach her eyes. They were still dark, and deep.

"Well," he said. "I bet if we asked really nice, and promised not to wrestle him for his hot dog, we could arrange a ride. Should we go say hi?"

In response, Ella jumped up to her feet and tugged on Bo's hand. He didn't even try to hide the smile on his face as they made their way across the lawn to Jeff. If she was excited about horses, that was one thing he could deliver. And if it was going to make her smile, well, he'd like that. Little girls shouldn't be so sad.

"Hey, Jeff." Bo tapped on his buddy's shoulder and the big man looked around away from the girls he was talking to.

"Bo!" He pulled Bo in for a manly hug-shoulder slap and released him with a fist pound. "How are you? Ready for another great summer? I hear there's a few really hot—"

"I want you to meet Ella," Bo interrupted. He gestured to

the little girl who was standing, mouth open, staring at the huge man. "My daughter."

"Your…" Jeff looked down, and then up, and then back down. "Your daughter, man? I had no idea."

"Neither did I," Bo muttered. He cleared his throat when Jeff gave him a strange look. "It's a long story. Anyway, I was just telling Ella here that you're in charge of the horses and it turns out that she really likes horses, so I thought maybe we could come see you at the stables some time." With his eyes, Bo tried to impart the importance of what he was asking to his friend.

The one thing Jeff liked more than women was horses. And Bo didn't need to ask twice. Jeff knelt in front of Ella and pointed to the clay deer in her hand. "Is that your horse?" He spoke softly, with a slightly childish tone and Bo had to check his look of surprise.

Ella nodded and galloped the statue through the air.

"I have a niece about your age," Jeff said. "She loves riding. Do you think you might like to come visit me at the stables soon and go for a ride? I bet I have just the right size pony for you to try."

Ella's head bobbed up and down so hard and fast that Bo had to let go of her hand. He watched while Jeff explained how many horses he had and how he had to brush them every day. Ella didn't say anything, but she hung on his every word. Every once in a while, she would nod or smile in response to something that Jeff said.

"Hey there, Bo." The voice distracted him from watching Ella, and Bo turned around to find Pam, a woman he'd met the season before, holding two bottles of beer. She held one out to him, which he took with a smile. They'd had a brief relationship, if you could call it that. Bo smiled with the memory of how much fun they'd had. But things were different then, he reminded himself before he got carried away.

"It's good to see you, Pam. How've you been?" He took a deep slug from the bottle. "Thank you," he said, nodding to the beer. "I hadn't thought to bring any."

"Well, I aim to please," Pam said with a wink. "I'm looking forward to the summer, aren't you?" Her sultry voice washed over him. Oh yes, he was— "Who's the kid?" Her abrupt question interrupted his thoughts.

"She's…" Bo glanced around quickly and took a few steps to the side so Ella wouldn't overhear. He looked cautiously at her, worried that she would be upset by the distance. He needn't have worried, though, as she didn't seem to notice, as distracted as she was by Jeff's stories.

Bo turned back to Pam, and said, "That's Ella, she's…" He lost his train of thought when a tall brunette on the other side of the campfire caught his attention. Her back was facing him, but he could see that she was laughing. There was something familiar about her, but he couldn't put his finger on it. She was probably someone he'd met last season, but there was something different about her, something more compelling.

Bo turned and said to Jeff, "Do you think you could keep an eye on Ella for a moment?"

"Of course. How do you feel about roasting a marshmallow?" Jeff asked Ella and with a happy nod they headed off together.

"Sorry, Pam," Bo said, turning back to the blond. "It was great seeing you, but I have to…"

She followed his gaze and laughed. "You haven't changed a bit," she said.

Pam took off in the opposite direction, and Bo stared after her. He had changed. At least, he thought he had. But there was something about the brunette he couldn't ignore. With a shrug, he took another swallow of his beer and navigated around the fire towards her.

"Excuse me," he said, and tapped the woman on her shoulder. She turned around and the smile on her face faded with a flash of recognition in her eyes.

Damn.

He realized a second too late why she looked so familiar.

Chapter Four

"BO, RIGHT?" Morgan tried to keep her voice controlled.

"Morgan," he said.

She nodded and crossed her arms over her chest. "Can I help you with something?" She tipped her head to one side and waited for the apology he owed her. Surely he didn't seek her out just to interrupt her for the second time in one day?

"I thought you were someone else," he said.

Morgan tried not to let the surprise on her face show. The nerve of this man. He'd been intolerably rude to her earlier, and it was clear that he wasn't going to be offering her an apology any time soon.

"Well," she said, trying her best to look calm. "I guess I'm not who you thought I was." She moved to turn back to the crowd she'd been chatting with. Astrid was eyeing her with a sly smile on her face.

"Wait," Bo said. "The least I can do is offer you a drink."

Morgan turned and looked at him again. He had the air of a man who knew how handsome he was. Too confident. Even though she'd sworn off men, she couldn't ignore the way his worn, soft blue jeans hugged his body. His t-shirt was tight on his arms and chest. Not too big like some of the men she'd seen already, but with the look of a man who was no stranger to physical labor. Strong. And arrogant, she reminded herself when she looked again to his face. His dark eyes were watching her intently, as if he, too, were trying to figure her out.

Well, keep trying, she wanted to say to him—I'm not interested.

"I have some," Morgan said, and pointed to the cooler on the ground next to Astrid.

"Well, let me get you one then."

Before she could object, Bo strode to the cooler and flipped it open. He selected a bottle and with a flick of his wrist, popped the top and returned to her. "Here you go," he said.

She frowned at him but took the drink. "Thank you."

They stared at each other for a few moments before Morgan broke the standoff by taking a sip of her beer. She didn't normally drink much and the few she'd already drunk had made her bolder than she might normally be.

"So," she said, keeping her voice as cool as she could, "I trust that you were able to figure out whatever situation you had earlier."

Something flashed across his face, causing him to lose his air of control for a split second. "I did," he said. His voice was softer than it had been. Bo gave his head a quick shake, causing one unruly dark lock to flop over his eye. Morgan squeezed her bottle to keep from reaching out and brushing it off his forehead.

What was wrong with her? He may be handsome, but this man was not only infuriating, but he was a man. He would only lead to heartache and frustration. Which meant she needed to steer clear of him if she were hoping to find a fresh start.

"That's good," she said, her voice much weaker than she

wanted it to be. Morgan cleared her throat. "It seemed rather important."

"It was," Bo said.

"Morgan." Astrid came to stand next to Morgan and wrapped her arm around her. "I see you've met Bo, our resident Casanova." She flashed a wicked smile at Bo before releasing Morgan to give him a friendly hug.

"It's good to see you, Astrid." Bo grabbed a handful of Astrid's tiny braids in his hand and let them fall to her back. "New look?"

"Always," Astrid said and stepped out of his embrace. "I see you've met my roommate."

"Roommate?" Bo's eyes flashed with something. Humor, maybe? "We have become acquainted, yes."

Astrid laughed. "Don't worry—I'll fill her in on all the stories later."

Attention piqued, Morgan lifted an eyebrow in question.

"Don't believe all of them," Bo said. "Only some are true." He winked at Morgan and turned his focus back to Astrid. "How've you been? What did you do with the off-season?" She couldn't help the irrational and totally annoying flare of jealousy she felt at his attention on her friend.

The two launched into a conversation about their winter months and what staff had returned for the summer, but Morgan only half listened. She kept her eyes on Bo. Morgan knew his type. Over-confidant, arrogant, and very aware of what type of effect he had on women. He was everything she didn't need in her life right when she was trying to start over.

"Excuse me," Morgan said. She lifted her hand in a slight wave and backed away from the pair, leaving Astrid and Bo to catch up. They were deep in conversation, but Morgan didn't miss the smile Bo gave her and the way his eyes seemed to see right through her.

Morgan tried to put him out of her mind as she picked her

way through the crowd, nodding at people and smiling. Most of the group seemed to know one another already, probably from previous seasons, but it didn't bother her because the vibe was warm and welcoming, and she didn't feel as if she were on the outside of anything. Passing the bonfire, Morgan stopped and watched a small blond child roasting a marshmallow. Her dad, one of the over-muscled men she'd seen earlier, smiled and laughed when the little girl withdrew her stick and revealed her flaming treat. She watched, frozen in place as he blew it out and offered the child his own perfectly roasted marshmallow.

The sweet scene had tears pricking at Morgan's eyes. She blinked hard and forced herself to move away so she wouldn't have to watch. She walked fast, trying not to run, until she got to the edge of the clearing and was alone. She looked up to the darkening sky and towering mountain peaks that were casting mysterious shadows in the early evening light and forced herself to gain some control. When would it get easier? When would the pain of seeing a child and knowing she'd never have her own lessen? It had been months since the doctor gave her the news, but still, she struggled with it.

She took a deep breath and let her lungs fill with air. She couldn't let herself get worked up. The doctor said that after dealing with such a serious case of endometriosis, even after it was under control—with the scar tissue that she likely still had —there was less than a five percent chance that she'd ever carry her own child. The odds were way too small to even consider. She took a few deep breaths and reprimanded herself. She was being ridiculous. The sight of one child should not send her into an emotional tailspin.

After a few moments, her heart rate calmed down and she wrapped her arms around her waist, hugging herself in defense of the coolness of the night that was starting to descend. She'd have to go back to the fire if she wanted to stay warm. Morgan turned back to the party, where it looked like things were starting to pick up. To her surprise, she wanted to go back and have some fun. Besides, it wasn't as if she could avoid children altogether.

She was just going to have to learn how to deal with her new reality.

As it turned out, Morgan didn't have to worry about running into the little girl again. By the time she returned to the fire, there was no sign of her. The little girl's father, however, seemed to have traded in his marshmallow roasting stick for another beer and was holding court with a group of girls. Just watching the sight, a sense of distaste settled around Morgan. It wasn't any of her business, but she couldn't help wondering what type of guy would bring a small child to a bonfire party and then dump her on a babysitter so he could pick up women. She could only assume that he'd even bothered to find a babysitter.

But it wasn't her business, and Morgan tried to remind herself of that as she grabbed another drink from the cooler and went in search of Astrid.

"Morgan," a voice yelled over the crowd. She turned to see Carmen pushing her way towards her. Carmen looked a lot different out of her work uniform. Much less intimidating, and a whole lot more fun with her black hair pulled into a high ponytail and her t-shirt untucked from her jeans. The beer in her hand helped with the image of fun, too.

"Hey there," Morgan said.

"Looks like you got settled in okay." Carmen waved her arm. "I'm really sorry about earlier. That's not how I usually like to handle staff orientation but Bo can be quite insistent and completely exasperating at times."

Morgan shrugged her shoulders and before she realized what she was doing, she scanned the crowd, hoping to catch a glimpse of the exasperating Bo. "It's fine, really," she said. "I met Astrid and she's been great. She's introduced me to lots of people and I'm sure I'll have no idea what all their names are tomorrow."

"Oh, good." Carmen's relief showed on her face. "That's one less thing for me to worry about. I can't tell you what a transition this new position has been for me. I'm not complaining or anything, but I think it's going to be a lot more challenging than I thought it would be."

"What do you mean?"

Carmen took a long pull on her beer bottle. "Oh, just trying to get all the staff here ready to work, and happy, of course." She took another slug on her bottle and Morgan raised her eyebrow in question. "Sorry," Carmen said, "I just need a little stress relief. You wouldn't believe how many last-minute openings I've had to fill."

"Really?"

"Oh, yeah and it's just the usual excuses. One got a job in the city, one guy got a position working in his field, and, oh yeah, now Patty's getting married. I just found out about that one yesterday."

Morgan offered a sympathetic smile. "That's terrible. And I can see how you might be a little stressed out. But at least you don't have to worry about me," she said. "I'm very happy to be here and thanks to Andi and Eva and Party Hearty, I have lots of experience with event planning. So my position is solid."

Morgan had been looking forward to the challenge of organizing a summer of weddings and family reunions up at the Lodge. Party Hearty would be called in for the larger events of course, but Morgan's job would be to ensure everything ran smoothly.

"Oh," Carmen said. "That totally reminds me. I need to

talk to you about your job this summer. I meant to bring this up earlier, but with the interruption and everything else that's been going on it totally slipped my mind."

"No worries. Is there a function or something I need to jump right into? I know I'm not meant to start until Monday, but I'd be happy to get right to work."

Morgan had been looking forward to exploring the trails and paths around the Lodge over the weekend, but the allure of jumping right into work was also a strong pull. Besides, she had all summer to explore.

"I'm glad to hear that you're willing to get to work, because I actually do need you to start tomorrow. But I had to shuffle things around a little and I was hoping you'd be willing to fill a different position."

Her attention piqued, Morgan crossed her arms and listened.

"I noticed on your résumé that you have quite a bit of experience with children. And actually with a degree in child development."

Morgan's stomach flipped. She was afraid she knew exactly what Carmen was going to say, and she didn't want to hear it.

"And Patty, the girl that's getting married," Carmen continued, "just left me high and dry in the Cub's Club. I think you'd be perfect for the position."

"Cub's Club?" Morgan was almost afraid to ask.

"It's for our child guests. It's much more than a babysitting room, which is why I think you'd be perfect for it. Patty did great things there. Crafts, games, activities. She used to…"

Morgan stopped listening as Carmen went on to describe the job in detail. Her mind focused on words like: children, babysitting, perfect. Her mind spun and for a terrifying moment when she couldn't focus on the woman in front of her, she thought she might pass out. How could she take a job working with children? The whole point of coming up to Castle Mountain was to escape.

"Morgan?"

She forced herself to focus. "Sorry," Morgan said. "I was just thinking."

"So you'll take it?"

"Actually, I really don't think I'd be right for the job."

Carmen's face fell and Morgan felt a flash of guilt. "Of course, you're perfect," she said. "Plus, you won't have to work any evenings unless the guests hire you for extra hours, which can be very lucrative."

Morgan swallowed hard and tried to look as professional as possible. "I'd really rather stick with the event planning ,if it's all the same to you."

"Actually," Carmen said, "there's really no other choice." She pressed her lips into a hard line. "The other position has been filled."

"Filled?" For the second time, Morgan's stomach flipped and she was afraid she might be sick.

"I honestly didn't think you would have any problem with the change. Besides, I didn't have any other choice. None of the other applicants have any experience with children, and then there was your résumé staring up at me."

"So I don't have a choice?" Morgan struggled to keep her voice calm.

The other woman shook her head. "No. I'm afraid you don't. It's the only opening left. I'm sorry, but I really thought you'd be happy with the change."

"No," Morgan said, her voice barely a whisper. "I really don't want to work with children at all. I'm going to have to think about this," she said.

"Think about what? The job?"

"Yes...I..." Morgan couldn't finish the thought, because she wasn't sure how to. A million thoughts raced through her brain. She'd already given up her apartment. She had nowhere to move back to if she went back to the city. And her job? Andi and Eva certainly would give her a job at Party Hearty, but the whole idea of going up to the Lodge was to give herself a fresh start. A chance to adjust to the idea that her future could never be what she thought it would be. It was one thing to see children now and then; it would be another thing entirely for her to spend her days surrounded by them.

"Please tell me you're going to do it," Carmen said, interrupting Morgan's thoughts. She drained her beer and stared at Morgan. After a moment, Carmen sighed. "I'm going to have to find someone else, aren't I?"

Morgan nodded slowly. "Yes," she said. "I'm sorry, Carmen. But I can't do it. I just can't work with children."

"You're sure? I told you, I don't have any other positions."

Morgan nodded again.

"Okay," Carmen said with a sigh, "but can you please at least work tomorrow? I'm kind of stuck until I have a chance to find someone else."

"I don't know—"

"Please, Morgan. There's only one little girl scheduled. It'll be easy."

Carmen looked as if she might cry, and despite the fact that Morgan felt as if she was going to either throw up or pass out at any moment, she nodded. "Okay. One day. Then I guess I'll go."

"Thank you," Carmen said. She grabbed Morgan and gave her a quick hug. "I'm telling you, the stress of this job is going to kill me. Come on, let's go get another drink."

Morgan did her best to smile, but she didn't follow as Carmen wove her way through the crowd. Looking around at the party going on around her, all the people she no longer would be working with for the summer, she didn't much feel like celebrating.

Chapter Five

BO TOOK one more look down the hall where he'd left Ella in the Cub's Club. She's in good hands, he reminded himself. Besides, Carmen said the Cub Counsellor would be there right away, and those people had experience with kids. Ella would be fine—probably better than fine. Maybe she'd even come out of her shell a little bit. It wasn't right that a little girl should be so sad.

When he'd left her, Carmen had been trying to get her to put down the ceramic deer, which she'd eyed suspiciously, but fortunately not commented on, and go play with some of the other toys. Ella certainly hadn't said anything, but Bo could tell she was a little overwhelmed. Didn't that make two of them?

His thoughts were still focused on Ella and how he might be able to make her smile when Bo walked through the lobby of the main lodge. He didn't see the woman running across the room until the last second.

He reached out and grabbed the woman to keep her from slamming into him. "Whoa," he said.

They spun in an awkward dance before she looked up into

his eyes. The expression in her eyes changed from shock to one of annoyance in a flash. "You," she said.

"It's me." He tried to keep the laughter out of his voice. "Morgan, right?" He released her and she immediately pulled at her shirt, trying to adjust her uniform. "You should watch where you're going. This place is going to get pretty busy soon," he said.

"Well, I'm sorry," she said. Was it his imagination, or was she hostile towards him? He couldn't remember doing anything, well, not much of anything anyway, to annoy her. "I'm late."

He stood back and swept an arm out to the side gallantly. "I should let you get going then. It wouldn't do to get in trouble on the first day."

She blushed, which Bo couldn't help noticing had the effect of softening her annoyance and making her look extremely beautiful.

"I don't know if it will matter actually," she said. "I'll be leaving on Monday."

The stab of disappointment that shot through him surprised Bo. "Leaving? But the season is just starting."

"Yes, well…" Morgan looked down at her feet and twirled the end of her ponytail around her finger. "I just don't think it's going to work out."

"That's really too bad," Bo said. "We got off on the wrong foot and I'm sorry about that."

Her head shot up; the annoyance that he was already used to seeing on her face was back. "I assure you that my decision had nothing to do with you."

Bo smiled. "I'm glad to hear it." He searched her eyes with his. She was a tricky one to figure out. He couldn't get a read on her. After a moment, he said, "I'll be sorry to see you go, Morgan."

Something flickered in her eyes but it was gone so fast, he

couldn't be sure that he saw it at all. "Well, I'm going to be late." She dodged around him and hurried across the room.

Bo watched her disappear down the corridor before turning to head outside. He had to walk some trails, and check conditions before the guests started to arrive. It wouldn't do to lead guests through muddy, snow-covered trails. Some liked them rough and rustic, but most didn't. And he wasn't going to be able to earn the types of tips he needed by leading a bunch of tourists down a soggy trail.

He headed out on the paved trails that led away from the Lodge. At least five kilometers of paved trails wound through the main buildings, around the pond in the courtyard, and along the mountain ridge. The entire area was accessible for all guests, including those in wheelchairs and pushing strollers. The accessibility was one of the things that made Castle Mountain so popular because there was something for everyone. He didn't have to check those trails to know that they'd be fine because the Lodge kept them in good condition all year round. He quickly veered off the pavement and on to Spruce Track—one of the easier hikes he liked to try the inexperienced hikers on before venturing further out.

Bo moved at a comfortable pace, hopping over exposed roots and rocks. He pulled his notebook out of his back pocket and recorded where trees had fallen and would need clearing, or areas that would be treacherous in less favorable conditions. The spring had been warm, and all of the snow on the lower trails was melted. But it wasn't the lower trails he was worried about. He was eager to get up on the mountain and lead a group to Lake of the Hanging Glacier. It was an all-day trek, and like the name suggested, the trail led to a breathtaking lake that was fed by a stunning glacier. A log cabin—they called it

Stanley's Cabin for the man who discovered it—at the top was perfect for overnight stops. He wouldn't have time to check the whole path yet but at least he could check out the trail head.

A rustle in the trees behind him caught his attention and Bo turned slowly with one hand on the canister of bear spray he kept on his hip. The mountains were full of cougars and bears, a fact that always stunned some guests when he went through his survival tips. It never failed to surprise him how many of the tourists thought those animals were only found in the zoo.

He squatted lower to the ground and listened for a moment before he stood upright again and laughed.

"You almost got me, Jeff," Bo called out.

A second later, Jeff appeared on horseback coming around the bend and through the trees. Besides his own black mare, he led two others.

"Hey," he said, "I didn't know you'd be out here this morning." Jeff hopped out of the saddle and landed on the ground with a surprisingly graceful thump.

"I've been itching to check out the trails," Bo said. "There'll be guests here before we know it and it'll be time to get out here."

"True enough." Jeff patted the mare. "That's why I wanted to get Sally out here. Thought I'd warm up a few others, too. I think the horses are just as excited for the season to get fired up."

"Let's walk for a bit." Bo gestured down the path.

Jeff fell into step next to his friend, leading the horses behind him. Together, they walked in silence for a few minutes. They knew each other well, and just being outside together in the woods was enough to strengthen their friendship after a winter apart. But it wasn't long before Jeff broke the silence.

"So," Jeff said as they approached the trail head. "Are you going to tell me about that sweet little girl you have?"

Bo sighed and rolled his shoulders back, releasing some of the tension he'd been holding. "There's not much to say. I didn't really have much of a relationship with her mother."

"Do you with any of them?" Jeff quipped and Bo shot him a look. "Sorry," Jeff added, "that was out of line."

"Anyway," Bo continued, "she doesn't have anyone else, and Tessa named me in her will. So, I got the call and a few days later, Ella."

"Wow, man. I can't even imagine." Jeff wiped his sleeve across his brow. "She's pretty cute, though," he said. "Must take after her mama, huh?" He dodged Bo's punch and laughed. "So what are you going to do? I mean, you can't keep her at the Lodge."

Bo stopped in his tracks and stared at his friend. "Why not?"

"It's not much of a place for kids, is it? I mean, it's good for holidays and all, but to live? That sucks, because rumor has it that they were going to offer you the full-time gig. You know, leading winter treks and all that. Isn't that the one you were after?"

Crap. With everything that had happened in the last few days, Bo'd forgotten all about putting in for the outdoor recreation manager position. He took a moment to digest what Jeff had said before he spoke again. "I don't think I can keep her anyway." At Jeff's confused expression, he quickly continued, "I mean, what kind of father can I be? And like you said, the Lodge is no place for a child to live, even if I could."

"I thought you said there was no where else for her to go?"

"There isn't...but—"

"You'd turn her over to Social Services? Your own daughter?"

"No!" Bo's response surprised even him. "No," he said again, calmer. "I mean, I don't want to. But they were looking into some family. An uncle, I think."

Jeff shook his head slowly. "Did I ever tell you I was a foster kid?"

Bo shook his head. Neither of them had ever really talked about their childhoods.

"It's a hard life for a kid," Jeff said. "Don't get me wrong. It's the right decision for some and I did end up with a really good family. Even got a few pesky little sisters out of the deal, but..." He looked past Bo, staring into the woods for a moment, lost in a memory.

"Jeff?"

His buddy shook his head, clearing the memory. "Sorry," Jeff said. "I was just thinking."

"So what do you think I should do?"

Jeff shrugged. "No idea. But you definitely need to think about it."

Bo kicked at a loose rock on the trail. "I've been doing nothing but. I mean, what if I keep her and screw it up?" Bo ran a hand through his hair. "I don't know anything about kids, and my situation is less than ideal. Maybe she'd be better off with a nice family. People who can provide her with a stable home and like you said, maybe some sisters and—"

"Is that really what you think?"

"I don't know," Bo answered truthfully. "That's the whole problem. I just don't know." But what Bo did know was that when he got back to the Lodge, he had a call to make. Maybe Clara Kersey could help him with an answer.

Chapter Six

IT WAS bad enough that she was late, but after her run-in with Bo, Morgan had to take a minute to compose herself before walking into the Cub's Club. Sure, he was arrogant and full of himself, but there was something else about him that made her blood run hot and for the second time in as many days, Morgan had to remind herself that she wasn't looking for a relationship, particularly with a man like Bo.

Morgan took a deep breath and opened the door. Carmen was waiting for her and just like she'd promised, only one little girl sat on the colorful carpet. The same beautiful, blond girl she'd seen at the campfire the night before.

As soon as she saw her, Carmen headed straight for Morgan. "Oh, thank goodness," Carmen said. "I was afraid you'd decided not to come at all."

"I'm sorry I'm late," Morgan said.

"Oh, it's fine. I knew you wouldn't do that to me. You're not the type," Carmen said. "You know you can always change your mind about the job."

Morgan held up her hand before Carmen got the wrong

idea. "I'll tell you what," she said. "I'm here now. Let's just leave it at that."

Carmen smiled apologetically. "You don't have to give me an answer right now."

Morgan was pretty sure that her answer wasn't going to be any different by the end of the day, but she didn't bother pressing the issue. Instead, she listened while Carmen gave her a brief run-down of the room and the amenities. Morgan had to admit, it was a pretty impressive child-care room and if she were still interested in a career in child development, she'd be jumping at the chance to work in such a space. But she wasn't. Not anymore. So instead of letting her mind run free with ideas and activities that she could conduct in such a place, she put a lid on them and instead focused on what Carmen was saying.

It didn't take long to get the complete tour and then it was time for Morgan to meet the little girl, who until that point had been drawing quietly in the center of the room.

"Normally, there would be a lot more children here," Carmen said. "And of course, a lot more staff. We like to keep a five to one ratio with the kids because that way we can really get to know them and have a lot more fun with them."

"Of course," Morgan said.

"Let me introduce you to Ella," Carmen said as she walked to the carpet. "She's the daughter of one of the outdoor recreation guys. Normally we don't have children of the staff in Cub's Club, but this is a special situation."

Morgan nodded and offered a small smile.

Together they walked to the table, but Ella didn't look up. "She's very quiet," Carmen said. "As far as I know, she's only spoken a few words to her dad, even. Her mother just died and—"

"I'll take it from here," Morgan cut her off abruptly and shot the other woman a look that she hope conveyed how utterly inappropriate it was to talk about a child as if she wasn't sitting right in front of you. She waited for Carmen to excuse herself from the room before crouching down at the table next to Ella.

"Hi there," she said and when Ella didn't even look up she added, "Looks like you're working on a really pretty drawing. Is it a horse?"

Ella tipped her head up and peered at Morgan through long blond lashes. Her dark eyes were wide, but still she didn't speak.

"I love horses," Morgan said gently. She reached for a piece of paper of her own and took a crayon from the bowl. Without saying anything, she slowly started sketching out the rough outline of a horse on her own paper. "Have you ever been on a horse, Ella?"

The little girl shook her head slowly.

"I have," Morgan admitted. "But not for a very long time." She turned her attention to her own drawing and after a moment, Ella returned to her project as well.

They sketched in silence for a few minutes before Morgan tried again. She reached out and pointed to the clay deer that sat on the table by the crayons. "Is this your deer?"

Ella's head popped up and she grabbed the deer, clutching it close to her chest. "Horse." Her voice was tiny and thin. Morgan tried to hide her excitement at hearing her speak.

"I suppose it could be a horse," Morgan said carefully. "They do look similar."

The little girl eyed her cautiously as she stroked the clay figure. It looked familiar but Morgan couldn't place it. Like something she'd seen in the lobby, maybe?

"You know what, Ella?" Morgan was struck with an idea. "Maybe there are some toy horses around here we could play with." She scanned the room, looking at the various bins and shelves full of toys and craft supplies. "I bet we could find some." Morgan hopped up and to her surprise, Ella followed.

Together, they searched through the baskets and buckets of surprisingly well-organized toys until they found a bin labeled "farm animals."

"Jack pot," Morgan declared and pulled the bucket out on the carpet. She upended it, spilling the contents of a variety of barnyard animals, including three plastic horses. Ella let out a high-pitched squeal and grabbed up the horses. Morgan busied herself, setting up the fences and the other animals while Ella galloped them around the carpet. She didn't want to say anything to break the spell that the little girl was under, so she took her time arranging the rest of the farm. After a few minutes, Ella looked up.

"Do you want to play with all the animals?" Morgan asked her.

Ella shook her head and clutched the horses to her chest.

"That's okay," Morgan said. "You don't have to. The horses are great. You just let me know if you want to play with anything else, okay?"

The little girl nodded and went back to her play. The clay deer seemed to be the "horse" in charge while the little plastic horses galloped around in circles. Morgan sat back and watched for a few minutes before she pushed up off the floor and started wandering around the room. While Ella played, Morgan snooped through the drawers, marveling at what she found. The Cub's Club was remarkably well-equipped, not only with a wide variety of toys, but also educational tools that would excite any child-care professional. Even though she had no interest in staying on, old habits die hard and Morgan couldn't help but let her imagination run free with all the programs she could run in such a space. Along one wall, she found a cabinet with books and binders that contained ideas for games, hikes, treasure hunts, and other activities that were obviously conducted at the Lodge.

She couldn't help herself; Morgan felt a thrill go through her. It wasn't just a babysitting room. Everything about the Cub's Club was exactly what she had hoped to be doing with her degree. Well, maybe not exactly, but if she were being honest with herself, planning parties wasn't what she wanted, either. Working with children was. It's all she'd ever wanted. She glanced to where Ella was playing quietly. The little girl clearly had some issues and only a few months ago Morgan would have been enthusiastic at the prospect of helping her work through them.

Morgan twisted a strand of hair around her finger and contemplated the idea. Could she bring herself to work with children every day when the truth about her own childlessness was still so fresh and hard to bear? The now-familiar twist in her stomach as she thought about all she'd never have flared up. "No," she whispered to herself. "I can't do it. It's too hard."

For the rest of the morning, Morgan tried to busy herself with tidying up the room that was already incredibly clean. She tried to get Ella to talk, but either the little girl was much more interested in her horses or she just didn't want to talk to a strange woman—probably both. Finally, around lunchtime, Ella got off the floor and stretched her legs. Morgan waited while she made her way across the room to her. Sometimes a child needed to make the first move. She waited, and eventually Ella approached her.

The little girl made a motion to her mouth.

"Are you hungry?"

Ella nodded.

"Can you tell me that you're hungry?"

Ella shook her head violently.

"I know you can tell me, Ella." Morgan spoke softly but firmly. "I've heard you speak, so I know you can."

Ella clamped her lips together, and her eyes widened, but Morgan didn't stop talking. "I know sometimes it's scary to say what you need to say and you might think I won't listen to you. But I will. I promise that whatever you say, I'll always listen. Even if it's just to tell me that you're hungry. And," she added, "talking is the best way to let everyone know what you want. Do you understand?"

She nodded and then just when Morgan thought it was a lost cause, Ella opened her mouth and said, "Lunch."

A smile split Morgan's face and she nodded in agreement. "It is lunch. Did your dad pack you a sandwich?"

Ella shook her head and Morgan raised her eyebrows. "No," Ella said, her voice tiny and quiet.

"Okay. So what do you say we go find something to eat?" Morgan stood and without offering, Ella slipped her hand into Morgan's. As a reflex, Morgan squeezed her small fingers tightly and she thought her heart might crack from the simple action. Her instinct was to pull away, protect herself from the pain. But when she looked down at Ella's dark eyes staring up through her blond fringe, she couldn't do it. The little girl looking up at her was hurting. And her own pain would have to wait, at least for the moment.

Together, they went in search of the dining room, and Morgan, unaware of the protocol for the Cub's Club, persuaded the kitchen manager to make them grilled cheese sandwiches, which they ate at a picnic table that overlooked the pond in the courtyard.

The rest of the day passed quickly, and soon Carmen reappeared at the door. "So?" she asked, glancing around. "How did it go?" Her gaze landed on Ella, curled up in the oversized cushions under the base of the large treehouse that sat against one wall. "She looks content."

"She is," Morgan said. "We played hard all day and she finally succumbed to a nap. It was a big day."

Carmen walked to Morgan, peering down at Ella as she passed. "She's a sweet child. It's a shame what she's been through."

Morgan bristled. She normally didn't like talking about a child's situation when they were in the room, but Ella was asleep, and she couldn't help her natural curiosity. "What do you mean?"

"Well, she's only just come to be with her father." Morgan remembered the man at the campfire the night before roasting marshmallows with Ella. "And she's only just met him. Her mother died unexpectedly about a month ago and left little more than a note, but the poor thing never even knew her father."

Ella was essentially alone, which would explain her communication issues. It must be terribly confusing for such a little child to lose her mother and get thrust into a new relationship with a man she didn't even know.

"Oh my," Morgan said. "I can't even imagine what she must be going through. Her unwillingness to speak is a classic response to a stressful situation." Morgan let her thoughts drift for a minute, going through the countless other symptoms that Ella might display. "You said this just happened recently?"

"Within the week," Carmen said. "As far as I know it was a one-night stand type of thing. I don't really know the details so I shouldn't really say too much more."

"No, you shouldn't." Both women turned in the direction of the voice.

***

Bo stood in the doorway, his arms crossed and his mouth pressed into a very tight, very angry frown. A sheen of sweat beaded on his forehead, and his shirt sleeves were rolled up despite the coolness outside. He had the undeniable look of a man who'd been putting in a hard day of physical work, and Morgan couldn't help the twinge of desire that shot through her when she looked at him. She immediately shut it down, which wasn't hard seeing how angry he was.

"Bo," Carmen started. Her face turned crimson and she fluttered her hands in front of her. "I was just—"

"Gossiping about my daughter," he said, finishing the statement for her.

His daughter? Morgan turned quickly between Bo and Ella trying to process what he'd just said. Wasn't the muscle-bound man from the fire Ella's father?

"And we'll be going," he said. He strode into the room and across the carpet to where Ella was just waking up. She sat up and put her fists to her eyes, rubbing the sleep out of them. Bo came to a stop in front of her and held out his hand. He looked much less confident than he had a moment before. "It's time to go, Ella." Morgan couldn't help but be impressed with the way he spoke to her. His voice had softened, despite his irritation with her and Carmen.

The little girl shook her head and clutched her clay deer to her chest.

"Ella," Bo said again, "we need to go."

She didn't answer, but pushed up from the floor, scattering the plastic horses on her lap. She ran to Morgan and wrapped herself around her leg.

Morgan felt her chest tighten and she reflexively put her arms around Ella. She looked down to the little girl, who had a remarkably strong grip on her. Just as her training had taught her, she looked into Ella's eyes. Morgan's time in various classrooms and working with troubled children had taught her that more often than not, if a child didn't want to go with her parents, there was a good reason. But no, when Morgan searched Ella's wide eyes, there was no fear contained in them. But there was something else. More of a look of bewilderment, which would make sense, given everything she'd been through.

"You work here?" Bo asked.

Morgan looked away from Ella to meet Bo's gaze. His arms were crossed tightly across his chest and he was openly staring at her. She could tell he was struggling to maintain his composure.

"Morgan was just filling in for us," Carmen said. "I'm afraid she'll be leaving us after today."

Ella squeezed Morgan's leg tighter and when she looked down again, the little girl's eyes were filling with tears. Slowly, Morgan pried Ella's fingers apart and crouched so she could look into her eyes.

"No," Ella whispered. "You stay."

"Ella, I—"

"Did she just talk to you?" Bo interrupted. "She doesn't talk. I mean, she does," he spoke quickly, his voice taking on a new urgency, "but she's only ever said a handful of words to me."

Morgan ignored him and kept her focus on the little girl. "It's okay, sweetie." She brushed away a tear that slid down Ella's cheek. "I'm right here."

"Don't go."

The frail voice broke Morgan's heart and she squeezed her own eyes tightly in defense. She couldn't stay. She knew that. She'd spent the entire day convincing herself it wasn't a good idea and mentally preparing for the trip down the mountain and back to the city. She couldn't change her mind, because of one child.

"You can't be serious," Bo's strong voice broke through her thoughts.

Behind her, Carmen spoke. "I'm afraid Morgan will be leaving the Lodge after her shift today," she said. "She's decided the job isn't for her. I've tried to persuade her to change her mind, but she won't stay."

"Try harder," Bo said. He spoke as if she wasn't in the room, just mere steps away. "You see how Ella is responding to her—she can't go. Offer her more money."

"Bo, I'm afraid I can't do that. I've—"

"You haven't tried," he growled. Morgan listened as his footsteps traveled the room, but still she didn't take her eyes off Ella.

"You know you'll be fine without me?" Morgan spoke quietly, so only Ella could hear.

The little girl shook her head violently and wrapped her arms around Morgan's neck. The room was silent except for Ella's slight sobs and then Bo's heavy steps moving back towards them.

"You're not leaving," he said.

Something in his tone, demanding and forceful, caused Morgan to pry Ella's arms away and turn around. "Excuse me?"

"There's no way you can leave," Bo said. "I'm not doing that to her." He pointed to his daughter, whose face was now buried in Morgan's shoulder.

Morgan looked up at him with his strong arms crossed over his broad chest, his dark hair tousled from a day spent outdoors and it didn't take much to realize that Bo was probably used to getting his way. He had the air of a man who didn't take no for an answer and hadn't she already experienced that firsthand?

Carefully, with Ella still attached to her, Morgan stood. Giving herself time to form her thoughts, and keep herself calm, she did her best to straighten her shirt while balancing the surprisingly light child on her hip. "I don't think you're in any position to tell me what to do." Morgan made sure to look him directly in the eyes when she spoke and she didn't miss the flash of humor, or maybe it was irritation, that sparked there.

"Ms.?"

"Pierce," Morgan offered.

"Ms. Pierce," Bo said with a cocky smile. "It's true that I'm not in a position to make you stay in your job, but maybe I can appeal to your humanity?"

"Is that what you're doing?" She glared at him, meeting his stare head on. The muscles low in her belly contracted and she was immediately annoyed with herself for reacting to him. She forced herself to look away and focus on Ella. "Remember that little fridge we found in the office?" Morgan pointed to the little administration room off the main Cub's Club space.

Ella nodded.

"Do you think you could show Carmen those popsicles we found there?"

Ella's face split into a smile, but it quickly faded and she clung tighter to Morgan.

"I promise not to go anywhere while you're gone," she said. "Okay?"

The little girl stared into Morgan's eyes as if searching for the truth. They were so much like her father's eyes, filled with the same intensity. Morgan waited until Ella nodded slowly and then she set her on the ground. She watched as Carmen took Ella's hand and together they walked across the room. It wasn't until they'd disappeared inside the office that Morgan turned back to Bo.

"Are you about finished?" She spat the question at him, surprising herself with her vehemence. "What makes you think I'd change my plans because you said the word? You may be used to getting who and what you want around here, but I can't be so easily swayed. I have my own reasons for leaving the Lodge and they don't include you or what it is that you want me to do."

Morgan jammed her hands in her front pockets but didn't back down. She waited for him to say something. It felt like forever but it could have only have been a few seconds. Finally, she watched as his face transformed into a sly smile.

"You aren't going to change your plans for me," he said. His self-confidence was starting to grate on her. "You're going to change them for her." He gestured to the office where Carmen and Ella still hadn't reemerged. "You like her."

"She's a sweet kid."

"You care about her," he said. "I can see it in your face. And thanks to chatty Carmen, I know you've heard at least some version of her story."

Morgan swallowed hard. She was all too aware that she was losing this battle of wills. "I don't want to work with children," she said. The moment the words were out of her mouth she wanted to grab them back. He didn't need to know her story.

Bo choked back a laugh and took a step closer to her. Morgan fought hard to control her breathing; every nerve ending was alert and on edge with his proximity, but she didn't dare step back. "Now, Ms. Pierce," he said, his voice low and deep but somehow not menacing in the slightest. "Is it me you're lying to? Or yourself?"

Morgan's breath hitched. There's no way he could know; no one did. But from the look in his eyes, it was clear that Bo had figured out that something was up. He was so close, she could smell him. A combination of pine and fresh air. If that was a cologne, they should bottle it. It clouded her thoughts and she struggled to maintain control. She was positive he'd be able to hear her heart racing but she refused to let him see how he affected her. Especially when she herself wasn't sure. She worked hard to still her racing thoughts and to figure out her next move.

"Stay," he breathed. She could feel the breath on her face as he spoke. His voice was softer, and despite herself, she met his gaze again. The hard, challenging eyes she'd seen a moment earlier were gone. Like his voice, they too were softer, almost as if they'd changed color. "Please," he said. "Stay." Bo reached between them and touched his hand to her cheek. His touch was brazen and far too intimate but it sent a thrill racing through her body, directly to her center.

She opened her mouth to speak. "I—"

"Morgan." Ella's voice surprised them both. Bo dropped his hand and they both took a step away from each other as Ella ran across the room and grabbed Morgan's leg with one sticky, popsicle covered hand. The other held the drippy, red treat. "You're here."

"Of course." Morgan smiled and glanced at Bo whose mouth was agape. Of course, if Ella had barely even spoken to him, it would definitely be unusual to hear her speak so clearly, let alone loudly.

After a moment, Bo regained his composure and mouthed the word *please* to her.

She glanced between them, father and daughter, and felt a tug that both excited and disturbed her at the same time. "Okay," Morgan said. "I'll stay." She spoke the last words to Bo directly and then, so there was no misunderstanding, she added, "For Ella."

Chapter Seven

BY THE THIRD day Bo had been taking Ella to the Cub's Club, he could already see a difference in her. She seemed happier, and more content. It was Morgan he had to thank for that. Ella really seemed to like her. And she wasn't the only one. The few times he'd seen Morgan since their confrontation, he couldn't ignore the pull he felt towards her. It wasn't like anything he'd felt for any other woman before, which both irritated and excited him. But his feelings or attraction, or whatever it was he was feeling for Morgan, didn't matter. What mattered was that Ella was happy. Or at least happier than she had been. And although Bo would never imagine that a little girl's happiness would ever mean so much to him, there was no denying that when Ella smiled, so did he. And she was smiling. Still not as much as he thought a four year-old should, but it was a start.

"Ella," Bo called from the kitchen. "Are you ready to go?"

She appeared in the hallway and ran towards him. The transformation that had taken place in only a few days was remarkable. Ella still didn't say a whole lot, at least not to him, and there was still so much he wanted to know about her. He made a mental note to ask Morgan whether Ella had opened up to her about anything.

Grabbing an extra pair of socks for his pack, Bo said, "We should get going—we don't want to be late." Ella nodded in agreement, and together they left their suite and headed down the path towards the main lodge.

Still early, the air hadn't had a chance to warm up yet. Bo zipped his jacket and glanced down at Ella to make sure she was warm enough. She only had a thin jacket, which she wore over the only sweater she had. It wasn't much, and it definitely wasn't suitable for the mountains. He'd have to get her some clothes if she were going to stay with him.

And there it was. The indecision he still felt about his own child pulled at him. He couldn't keep her. It was ludicrous to even think he could. But there was nowhere else for her to go. Except for the uncle. Maybe if Bo could reach him, and explain the situation, he might consider taking her in. Surely that was a better living situation for a little girl?

The thought twisted his gut, but Bo ignored it. He kicked at the ground. "Hey," he said to Ella, "let's hurry so we don't get cold. Wanna race?"

Her eyes lit up with the challenge and she sprinted forward. Bo stifled a laugh. She was competitive, just like her mother used to be. He had a flash of memory: Tessa beating him at a game of pool. The same glint in her eyes then that he'd just seen in Ella. That was how they'd met. In a bar, where she'd hustled him and he'd taken her home. Hardly a romantic story, but it never was where he was concerned, and Tessa hadn't been any different. Except she had, he thought. Tessa had been different because she had Ella.

A sharp cry interrupted Bo's memory and brought the present, and Ella, sharply into focus.

Ella was lying on the dirt path, clutching her knee to her

chest. Bo sprinted to her and dropped to the dirt. "Where does it hurt? Are you okay?"

Ella didn't answer, but pointed to the hole in her pants, and the stain of blood that was starting to seep through her jeans.

His stomach flipped at the sight and his head pounded. He'd seen lots of injuries—heck, he was trained in field first aid. Bo's hand fluttered over her little body, not landing in any one place. He couldn't remember his training. What if it were broken? Maybe he shouldn't move her. Was it a cut? "Come on," Bo finally said. He scooped her up and stood. Feeling her shiver in his arms, he pulled her closer and headed for the Lodge.

Bo burst through the doors of the Cub's Club and rushed through the room to the pile of pillows at the base of the climbing tree. He placed Ella carefully on a large pillow and propped up her head with another one.

"Morgan," he called. His eyes searched the room, frantic. "I need your help." Bo turned his attention back to his daughter, who was no longer crying, but staring at him with wide eyes instead. She sniffed and wiped her nose with the back of her hand. "Does it still hurt?" he asked her.

Ella nodded.

"Morgan!" Where was that woman? Ella was bleeding and she was nowhere to be found. What kind of child-care center were they running? He glanced around the room again and caught sight of Morgan as she appeared from the office. "Where have you been?" he barked at her.

When she saw Ella lying on the pillow, Morgan dashed towards them. Bo didn't miss the glare she shot him as she sank to her knees next to the little girl.

"What happened, sweetie?" she spoke softly to Ella and

dabbed at the new tears that had reappeared on Ella's cheek with a tissue that she miraculously produced. She didn't wait for an answer, but continued to talk in a soothing voice. "It looks like you have a little owie. Did you scrape your knee?" Ella nodded. "Well, it doesn't look terrible," Morgan continued, "but why don't we take a look."

"I don't know," Bo interrupted. "Maybe we should get a doctor. Or someone qualified in first aid."

"Aren't you qualified in first aid?" she shot at him and it looked a little as if she were smiling at him. "Bo," she spoke slowly. "You need to calm down. It's just a scrape."

Was she serious? For a moment, he wanted to yell at her, to demand they call a doctor. But he took a deep breath and looked back at Ella and her bloody knee. No, of course it wasn't really serious.

"Are you okay?" Morgan asked him.

Bo nodded but his stomach churned and he felt as if he might throw up. The room spun and he reached out to grab something, anything that would stabilize him. He grabbed Morgan's shoulder.

"Maybe you should be the one lying down," she said. He caught the touch of humor in her voice.

"I'm fine," he managed to choke out.

She gave him a look. The type of look that meant, yeah right, but thankfully she didn't say any more. Instead, she went back to tending Ella's cut. She rolled up her jeans and with expert hands, she washed the wound, which he had to admit, was little more than a scrape. She gently removed the dirt from the skin and applied a salve of some kind before pasting on a bandage

"There," Morgan said, "good as new." She pulled Ella's pant leg back into place. "But it looks like you'll need some new pants."

She pointed to the hole and Bo nodded.

"And, Bo," Morgan was still talking, "these shoes are totally inappropriate for the mountains. And if I'm saying that, it's really bad."

She was right. Ella needed new pants and new shoes, and some toys, he thought, looking at the ever-present clay deer clutched in her hand.

"You're right," he said. "She needs a lot of things." Things I can't give her, is what he wanted to say, but didn't.

Morgan looked at him for a beat, her eyes questioning him. She turned back to Ella, who was staring up at both of them. "All better, kiddo?"

Ella nodded.

"I thought so," Morgan said. "Why don't you go and pick out a game that we can do later? There's some new kids coming today and I thought it might be a good way to get to know everyone."

Eager to please, Ella jumped up, and without favoring her sore knee at all, went in search of the puzzles and games.

When she was out of earshot, Morgan turned to him. "Do you want to tell me what that was all about?"

"What?"

She tipped her head at him and raised an eyebrow. "Don't play dumb," she said. "I don't have time. But I have never seen a grown man react to a little cut like that. Especially one that's trained in advanced first aid. You do realize that kids get hurt, right?"

"Of course I know that." Bo crossed his arms. He did know that, but what he couldn't tell her was that when he'd seen Ella hurt, it'd just about killed him. He'd had no idea what to do. He felt helpless. But he couldn't tell Morgan that. "And I didn't freak out."

"Whatever you say. But you should probably make sure you have a first aid kit close by. Kids do have a tendency to need a lot of bandages. Even quiet little girls."

"Maybe I should," he admitted. Along with a lot of other things, he thought. "I'll put it on the list," Bo muttered under his breath.

"Pardon?"

"Nothing." He cleared his throat and relaxed his posture. "I was just thinking of some things I need to do."

Morgan tidied up the leftover supplies and stood. She was standing close, but he didn't move. And she smelled good. His gut tightened in response. Was it cherries? No, something else. Less fruity. But nice.

"Are you okay, Bo?"

The question caught him off guard, and he took a step back. He knew it was a bad idea to act on whatever feeling it was that he was having for Morgan. Especially as he was pretty sure that she thought he was a total jerk. He was aware of the fact that he'd been a total ass to Morgan when they first met and he couldn't figure out why. Probably because she didn't fall all over herself like every other woman at the Lodge. In fact, if it weren't for Ella, Morgan wouldn't have anything to do with Bo at all. It bothered him. And it intrigued him. But he still couldn't figure out what it was about her that put him on guard.

Before he could answer, Morgan added, "I mean, are you okay with Ella? It must be overwhelming, and I just wanted you to know, that—"

"I don't need your help," he snapped. He regretted his words as soon as he spoke them; she was just trying to be nice. But it was too late. The softness in her face was gone, replaced by the hard expression she normally reserved for him. "I'm sorry," he mumbled.

"Don't be." Morgan turned away. "Obviously you have it all under control."

He wanted to say something else. For a moment, Bo even wanted to spill his guts and tell her that he most certainly did not have it under control. That he didn't know the first thing about a little girl, or how not to freak out when she tripped, or what she should be wearing, or even where to get her more clothes. He wanted to tell Morgan that he'd panicked and called Clara Kersey at Social Services again and maybe, just maybe, she could find a better situation for Ella, something more stable and better suited for a child. He opened his mouth to tell her everything but before he could, he felt a tug on his pant leg.

Ella peered up at him. Her brown eyes peeked out from under her long bangs. She needed a haircut on top of everything too.

"Ella," he asked, crouching so he could hear her if she spoke. "What is it?"

"Can Morgan come for dinner?" It was the longest string of words Ella had ever said to him, and she'd asked the question so quietly, that for a moment Bo hoped he had misheard her.

"I'm sure Morgan already has plans tonight. We wouldn't want to—"

"I'd love to."

Bo stood and stared at her. Morgan smiled innocently before turning and walking away.

He opened and shut his mouth and then looked down at Ella, who he could have sworn gave him a conspiratorial smile.

Chapter Eight

EVEN AS SHE changed her clothes, Morgan still couldn't figure out what had possessed her to accept Bo's invitation. If you could even call it that. It was more like Bo trying to convince Ella that she wouldn't want to go, which was probably the only reason Morgan had accepted. She wasn't normally so antagonistic towards people, but there was something about Bo that brought out a challenge in her.

It didn't matter, anyway; she'd accepted and even if she wanted to, Morgan would never cancel, so she might as well make the best of it. She looked in the mirror and applied another coat of mascara. Besides, she wasn't interested in Bo. Was she? Maybe if she kept telling herself that, eventually she'd believe it. If things were different, if she were different, she would definitely be interested in him. Very interested.

She tossed the mascara tube into her makeup bag and picked up the lip gloss before putting it back. "No," she said to her reflection. "I will not make an effort."

"An effort for what?" Astrid popped her head into the bathroom and eyed Morgan's reflection in the mirror. "Where are you going all dressed up?"

"I'm not dressed up." Morgan smoothed her hands down her dress.

"Really? So you're just wearing a dress around here then?" Astrid leaned back against the doorframe and smirked at her. "Not that I don't appreciate it."

"Stop it." Morgan pushed past her friend and went out to their small living room. The scent of incense burning on the coffee table tickled her nose. "I'm going for dinner."

"With?" Astrid asked, following her down the hall.

"Ella asked me." Morgan grabbed her purse and busied herself by digging through the contents.

"Whoa." Astrid didn't even try to hide her shock. "So you're having dinner with Bo?"

"I assume he'll be there," Morgan said. She pulled a plain lip balm from her purse. "Ella's only four. I can't imagine that she can cook."

"So how exactly aren't you making an effort?"

"I'm not putting on lip gloss, if you must know."

"Wow." Astrid laughed. "You're right, putting on lip balm instead of lip gloss will really show Bo that you're not interested."

Morgan frowned at her. "I'm not interested," she said. Even to her own ears the words weren't convincing. "He's been nothing but a jerk to me since I've met him."

"He's still hot."

"I'm not into rude men. I'm not into any men," she said. "I told you before that I didn't come here to meet anyone."

Astrid moved in front of her, so Morgan couldn't look away. She held her hands up in a triangle. "Your aura is definitely giving off some strong vibes," she said. "But I still don't get you," she said. Her voice was soft and her eyes were searching for something that Morgan wasn't going to give up. "Half the men here are into you," Astrid continued, "but you don't even notice and then Bo asks you for dinner and you treat it like you're headed to a jail sentence. Well, except for the dress," she added with a wink. "And the heels."

For a second, Morgan considered telling her friend the truth. But when she couldn't even sort out her feelings in her own head, it probably wasn't a good idea to go around telling others about them. Instead, she tossed a throw pillow at her. "Whatever," Morgan said, trying to keep her voice light. "I just thought the dress would be nice, but it's not a date or anything. It's for Ella. She wanted me to come, and I couldn't say no to her."

"She is pretty sweet," Astrid agreed. She put the pillow back on the couch and went to the fridge, grabbing herself a beer. "And she seems pretty attached to you. But I thought you didn't like kids."

Morgan's stomach knotted with the familiar ache. "I'm going to be late," she said.

Before Morgan could reach for the door handle, Astrid's voice stopped her. "Hey," she said. "I know you don't want to talk about it, but whatever you're running from…" Morgan froze but didn't turn around. "Well, sometimes those are the things we should be running towards."

Morgan felt the prick of tears threatening in her eyes, but still she couldn't turn around. She slung her purse over her shoulder. "I'll keep that in mind," she said and, with a wave in Astrid's direction, she left, closing the door behind her.

She'd become pretty good at pushing her feelings aside. Or at least she thought she had. But the truth was, spending her days surrounded by kids at the Cub's Club wasn't nearly as hard as she'd thought it would be. Because Astrid was right—Ella was attached to her. But what Astrid didn't realize was that Morgan was becoming just as attached.

The walk from the staff residence to the row of guest suites where Bo and Ella were staying was long enough for Morgan to collect her thoughts, but not long enough for her to properly prepare for the evening ahead. She had no idea how she was supposed to make polite conversation with a man who both aggravated her and compelled her at the same time. But maybe it wasn't too late to cancel. She could go back to the apartment and call his suite. Better yet, she could get Astrid to do it. To say she'd come down with some sort of cold or flu or something. Anything.

But when Morgan thought of little Ella and how disappointed she'd be, all thoughts of canceling were out of the question. The poor child had been through enough heartbreak to last a lifetime, and Morgan wasn't about to be responsible for causing Ella any more pain. Even if it was just a cancelled dinner.

She stumbled along the rocky path. Heels had been a bad idea. When she tripped for the third time, Morgan almost took them off. Even if she insisted she wasn't trying to make an effort in her appearance, she had to admit that it did feel good to put a dress on again. Paying more attention to her footing so she didn't sprain an ankle, Morgan still managed to enjoy her surroundings.

The free-standing condo-style suites that Castle Mountain Lodge had were stunning. The sloping roof lines and cedar boards gave them a rustic chateau feel that blended into the woodsy surroundings perfectly and the imposing front doors looked as if they'd been hand-carved from old-growth trees. There weren't many windows on the front sides of the suites, which was done purposely to give the residents privacy. All the windows were at the back, where the real view was.

Morgan approached number three, noticing how the number was created from stone and positioned into the siding.

She took a deep breath and rapped on the door with the wrought iron door knocker. No turning back.

As soon as the door flew open and Morgan set eyes on Ella, her hair pulled back into a lopsided ponytail, with smudges on her dress, she could no longer remember why she'd wanted to cancel.

"Hi, kiddo. Am I early?"

"No," Ella said. "But…" she pointed behind her, "he's having trouble."

Morgan tried not to laugh. "Trouble with dinner?"

"Yup."

Morgan stepped into the suite and tried not to be too impressed with her surroundings. Just as she'd thought, there was a wall of windows along the back that offered the most breathtaking view of the mountains she'd ever seen. Somehow they looked even more impressive through the windows than they did when she was standing outside. "Maybe we should go see?"

Ella took her hand and together they went down the small hallway and into the great room with the small kitchen off to one side. Bo, unaware of her arrival, had his back turned to them and was frantically stirring something in a pot that smelled vaguely like spaghetti sauce, but she couldn't be sure.

"Ella, you should probably go get changed. She'll be here soon." Bo spoke in their general direction.

Morgan opened her mouth to speak, but Ella's giggle gave them away before she could.

Bo spun around, spoon in hand and tomato sauce splattered across the kitchen. "Damn," he muttered.

Morgan raised her eyebrows and gestured with her head towards Ella who didn't seem affected by her father's language choices. "Hi, Bo," she said.

"Hi." He grabbed a cloth and started wiping up the spills. "You don't have to look so amused."

Morgan didn't even try to hide her smile. "Do you need some help?"

"I have everything under control," he said, returning to the pot, which was now bubbling over. "Dammit."

"Language," Morgan said as sweetly as she could.

"Sorry," he mumbled.

Ella giggled again and Morgan shook her head. "Maybe I'll take Ella and get her cleaned up."

Bo turned around, this time without the spoon, and said, "Thank you. I'm sure I'll have everything finished up by the time you're done."

"There's no rush," she said. "Really, I hope you didn't go to any trouble."

Bo shrugged his shoulders. "It's all trouble when it comes to cooking. But I'm learning. Slowly." He smiled then, and Morgan could feel some of the tension leave the room.

She returned his smile and had the undeniable urge to reach across the eating bar that separated them to wipe a drop of sauce off his cheek. Thankfully, before she could make a fool of herself, Ella tugged on her hand.

"Okay," Morgan said slowly, trying to regain control of her senses. "We'll be back in a few minutes then."

It didn't take long to find something for Ella to wear. In fact, as far as Morgan was concerned, it didn't take nearly long enough. The child didn't have much to wear, and what she did have was mostly dirty. Surely Bo must know that she needed more clothing? A little girl should have a closet full of dresses and pretty tops to choose from. Morgan adjusted Ella's sweater to hide the stains on her t-shirt, and after locating a comb, started picking through the tangles on her head.

While she worked, Morgan chattered on about some of the

other children that were scheduled to join the Cub's Club in the coming days. "Maybe we can go on a nature hike," she said. "That sounds fun, doesn't it?"

Ella nodded.

Truthfully, the idea of a hike was more intimidating than appealing to Morgan. She hadn't had a chance to get out and explore the trails at all. And even if she had, she likely would have gotten lost. The closest she'd ever been to a trail was a path through a city park. Morgan made a mental note to ask Bo about some appropriate paths. There must be something close to the Lodge that would give the children the idea of being out in the wilderness without really venturing too far.

"Maybe your dad can help?" Morgan voiced the question aloud.

Ella still didn't say anything, but she never did when it came to Bo.

With most of the knots picked out, Morgan smoothed Ella's blond locks with her hand. "How would you feel about a braid?" she asked.

Instead of answering her, Ella tipped her head down. Morgan waited for a beat and then, as gently as she could, asked, "Do you want a braid, Ella? You have to tell me. It's okay to use your words, you know?"

Morgan moved around her so she was kneeling in front of Ella. She reached out and tipped up Ella's chin so she was looking at her. Silent tears spilled from the little girl's eyes and the familiar clench in Morgan's stomach tightened but she ignored it, focusing instead on Ella. With her thumb, she softly wiped Ella's tears from her cheek. "It's okay to cry, kiddo," Morgan said. "Do you want to talk about it?"

Ella shook her head and stuck her thumb in her mouth.

"Okay," Morgan said. "Do you want me to stop doing your hair?"

Almost as fast as it went in, Ella's thumb popped out of her mouth. "No."

Morgan smiled and moved behind her again. She moved the comb easily through Ella's hair. "Your mommy used to do this, didn't she?"

Ella made a sound that was a cross between a sob and a choke. But she nodded.

"And I bet you really liked it when your mommy did your hair," Morgan continued, "didn't you?"

Ella nodded again. A tear fell on her jeans, making a small wet spot. Morgan's heart broke a little bit, but she trusted in her training, and kept going.

"When your mommy did your hair, what was your favorite style?"

It took a few seconds, but Morgan was patient. She kept methodically stroking Ella's hair, using the comb to lift and separate the strands.

"A braid." Ella's voice was soft but clear.

"Would you like me to do a braid for you now?"

Surprising Morgan, Ella spoke again. "Yes," she said. "Please."

Morgan smiled to herself. It wasn't a big thing, but it was something. And for a child who'd been wounded as deeply as Ella, it was huge. Without asking any more questions, Morgan carefully braided her hair and by the time she finished, Ella's tears had stopped.

Chapter Nine

"DO YOU TALK ABOUT HER MOTHER?" Morgan asked.

The question was so unexpected that Bo almost spat out his coffee. They'd finished dinner, which had been pleasant enough and actually much more palatable than Bo had expected. While they ate, Bo actually found himself relaxing around Morgan and he'd enjoyed watching Ella light up when Morgan spoke about some of the activities she'd planned for the Cub's Club. It still surprised him every time Ella spoke—she did so little of it with him. But the sound of her voice was enchanting, and he'd be happy to hear it all day.

Bo swallowed his coffee and glanced to where Ella was watching television. "No," he said answering her question, "I wouldn't know what to say."

"You could talk about the things she liked, what she did for fun, and maybe even what she looked like," Morgan said. "It's good for Ella to keep her memories fresh and she needs to know that it's okay to talk about her, and of course to cry if she needs to."

They'd been getting along so well, it even seemed to Bo

that Morgan might actually like him, or at the very least, not find him completely irritating. But Bo had a sinking feeling that she was going to change her opinion of him once again when she heard the truth about his relationship with Tessa. He took a deep breath. There was no point hiding it. He needed this woman's help. "I can't talk about her mother," he said.

Morgan raised an eyebrow in question, but waited for him to continue.

"I can't talk to her about Tessa, because I didn't really know her."

"But she's your daughter's mother. How could...oh," Morgan said as realization dawned.

He was sure she'd make a smart comment about his reputation or about how he should be ashamed of himself. He looked down at his mug and waited.

"That's sad," Morgan said. Her voice was quiet and her comment so unexpected that Bo jerked his head up. "For Ella, I mean. It must be incredibly hard to lose your mother and then not be able to talk about her."

Bo's stomach dropped and for a second he thought he might be sick. He'd been so concerned about how Ella's presence was going to fit into his life that he'd barely given any thought to what she must be going through.

"I can't believe it," he choked out the words. "I haven't even thought about it." He ran a hand through his hair and looked over at his daughter again. He still hadn't gotten used to the idea that she was his daughter, but that was the reality of it and no matter what the long-term plan was going to be, that would never change.

"It's okay, Bo," Morgan said. "You're new to this, too." She reached out and put her hand on his. The warmth of her touch permeated him and he looked up into her eyes. "It's going to be okay," she said. "I can help."

He stared at her for a few moments. Her blue eyes drew him in. He was a drowning man, and whether he deserved it or not, she was extending him a life raft. "Thank you," he said. "I'd really appreciate it."

Morgan smiled and withdrew her hand. Instantly, he wanted it back.

"The first thing you have to do is take care of her clothing situation." She looked him straight in the eye and for some reason, he felt chastised. "The poor thing doesn't have the appropriate clothing, and she really doesn't have much of it at all. Are her things being sent?"

Bo glanced around the room before answering. "As far as I know, that's everything she has," he said, and as he spoke he realized how little he really did know. "That's all she had when, well, when I got her."

"No toys? Nothing?" Morgan's brows were furrowed as she questioned him. As if she were making mental notes.

"Nothing," Bo affirmed. "And I'll be honest, I don't know the first thing about what she might need. I realize she doesn't have everything, but I don't really know how long—" He'd been about to tell her that he still wasn't sure that having Ella live with him was the best solution, and that he'd been in touch with Social Services again, but something stopped him. "I don't know how long the weather will be cool," he finished lamely.

She tipped her head, looking at him quizzically. "Well, maybe I can help you make a list of things she might need. Can you have them shipped to the Lodge?"

He nodded. Regardless of how long Ella stayed with him, or if she stayed with him, she would still need some new clothes. It was the least he could do.

"More coffee?" he asked in an effort to distract his thoughts. She nodded and Bo stood up.

Ever since he'd made the call to Clara Kersey, he'd tried not to think about what he'd done. Clara had said that she'd try to get ahold of Tessa's brother on the East Coast again. Maybe he was in a better situation to take care of her. He'd tried to assure himself that she'd be fine with a family member. And maybe her uncle did have a more stable home. There had to be a better situation for her than living with him. Bo shook his head clear of the thoughts that continued to plague him. The truth was, he couldn't be sure that he'd made the right choice by calling but every time he thought about it, he was sick to his stomach. He grabbed the coffeepot and returned to the table.

"There's one more thing," he said as he poured her a fresh cup.

"What's that?"

He watched as she poured cream on to her spoon before tipping it into her mug. "How do you get her to talk to you? She barely says anything to me."

Morgan swirled her spoon in her coffee and put it in her mouth for a moment before resting it on a napkin. Bo had to look away.

"It's complicated," she said. "When it comes to children who've experienced a trauma the way Ella has, it's very common for them to retreat within themselves as a coping mechanism. It can take a while for kids to process what's happened to them, and to accept that their lives have changed. Especially with a child like Ella who has been thrown into a completely different situation with a stranger." She hesitated over the word, but Bo nodded his head in agreement. He was a stranger to Ella.

"So what can I do?" he asked.

He followed her gaze as she turned to look at Ella, now curled up in a ball, watching a cartoon. He should probably get her to bed, but he hadn't been keeping to any kind of bedtime schedule and it probably wouldn't hurt if she fell asleep on the sofa.

"You're lucky," Morgan said, when she turned back to him. "Ella's a smart and sensitive kid. I think she really wants to form a relationship with you."

He shrugged but secretly the idea both thrilled him and scared him. He wouldn't be able to have any kind of relationship with her if she left. "I don't know about that," he said. "But she really seems to have bonded with you."

"It's probably because I'm a mother figure for her. I'm assuming that I'm roughly the same age that Tessa was?"

Bo nodded.

"And I'm in a position of authority, and I take care of her. It's not unusual that she's bonding to me." Morgan lifted the mug to her lips and took a tentative sip.

"Still," Bo said. "It's a good thing. Ella needs that right now."

"She needs you, too, Bo."

"I don't—"

"She does." Morgan set her mug down again. "You want to know how to get her to open up? Talk to her. Ask her questions. And not ones that she can answer with a nod of the head. Spend time with her—she needs you. And more than that, she wants to be with you."

Bo looked down. Morgan would have no idea how her words had just knifed into him. The thought that Ella needed him in any serious way unsettled him. To be in charge of another life was a huge responsibility. Particularly when you were as ill-prepared as he was.

"Okay," he said after a moment. "I'll try." He looked up into her eyes. They were soft and kind, and for the first time, Bo felt as if he really did have some support with his crazy situation. There were still so many unanswered questions and still so much he wasn't sure of, but for the first time Bo felt as if he might have a shot at raising Ella and maybe, just maybe, with a little help, he'd be able to tell Clara Kersey he had everything under control.

———

They sipped their coffee for a few moments, enjoying the quiet companionship. Morgan broke the silence. "So," she said, looking up from her mug. "Maybe if I help you out with Ella, you could help me out with something?"

Bo's mind immediately flashed to all kinds of things he could help her out with, none of which was appropriate to discuss at the table. He tried to push those thoughts from his head and focus on what she was saying. "Of course. But what could you possibly need help with?"

She smiled, and there was a flicker of shyness peeking through her normally confident demeanor. "You're going to laugh," she said.

"I promise I won't." Bo reclined in his chair, enjoying seeing her so relaxed.

"I was hoping to take the Cub's Club out for a nature hike. The weather's beautiful and I hate to keep them cooped up indoors all the time."

"That doesn't sound like a problem."

"Well," Morgan hesitated. She grabbed a strand of hair and twisted it around one finger. "The thing is…I'm used to taking kids out to a park where there are fences, and the worst thing I have to worry about is a few scraped knees."

"And you're an expert with those," Bo interjected.

"Thank you." Morgan blushed. "But I'm kind of a city girl and I don't know the first thing about the outdoors. Truthfully, the thought of taking children anywhere near the forest terrifies me. So I really need your help."

Bo tried not to laugh. She looked so cute when she was

flustered and he got the impression that Morgan didn't ask for help very often. "I'd love to show you some trails that are good for kids."

"Oh…"

"What?" He eyed her, waiting for the rest of the favor.

"I was kind of hoping you could come along." She twisted her hair around another finger. "Kind of like a miniature guided hike. You could point out some of the plant life and maybe any other things…"

"Like wildlife?"

Morgan blanched.

He couldn't help it, Bo laughed. "Don't worry. If we're lucky, we might see some squirrels and maybe a deer or a rabbit."

"But no…you know?"

"Bears? Cougars?"

Morgan's face turned an even paler shade of white, if it were possible.

"No," Bo said quickly, trying to end her panic. "It's not likely that we'd run into any major wildlife if we stick close to the Lodge and make lots of noise. Which probably won't be a problem with a group of children." He smiled, trying to get her to relax. "But the big animals are definitely out there. And not really all that far away, so it's important to use common sense."

"But we'd be safe?" Morgan asked. "I can't take a group of children out into the woods if there's a real danger."

"We'd be safe," he assured her. "You really haven't been into the woods before?"

She pressed her mouth into a firm line and shot him a look. "There's nothing wrong with that."

Bo suppressed his grin. "No," he said. "Nothing. But you don't know what you're missing. And I can't wait to show you how amazing the outdoors can be. So much better than the city."

As Morgan relaxed into her chair and picked up her coffee mug again, Bo realized that he, in fact, couldn't wait to show her the outdoors. Anything, if it meant spending more time with her.

Chapter Ten

FOR THE SECOND time that afternoon, Morgan checked her list. She had only five kids in the Cub's Club today, and one extra staff member to help. The season was still gearing up, so it was a good time to try out the trail hike.

"Don't forget to stock up the first aid kit, Lisa," Morgan called to her staff. "We don't want to run out of bandages."

Lisa smiled at her, but Morgan didn't miss the eye roll as the other girl looked away. So what if Morgan was being extra careful? She'd done a lot of things with children before. Taken them on field trips to the zoo, painted clay pottery, and even gone to a swimming pool. But she'd never ventured out into the wild with them. If she were being a little paranoid, well, that was better than not being prepared.

Ever since Bo agreed to help her with a hike, Morgan had spent her evenings thinking of creative and fun ideas that they could incorporate into the day. She'd also spent a great deal of time thinking of all the potential things that could go wrong. She'd tried not to listen to the other residents of staff housing when they were telling stories of their own run-ins with the wildlife around the Lodge, and she'd done her best to ignore

Astrid, who thought it was hilarious that she'd never been on a hike before.

Everyone else seemed to think it was funny that she was like a fish out of water when it came to anything remotely outdoorsy, but she was trying. And even if she hadn't wanted to be in charge of children, Morgan had enough pride to do the best job that she could. Even if it meant venturing way out of her comfort zone.

"Miss Morgan," a voice distracted her from her thoughts. She looked down to see a little boy, about six, looking up at her with big eyes.

"Yes, Zak," she said, quickly reading his name tag. "What can I do for you?"

"My mom said we were going on a hike," Zak said. "Are we? 'Cause I like outside better."

Morgan smiled. She still couldn't believe that none of the parents had any concerns when she'd told them about the hike. They'd all thought it was a great idea. And it was, she reminded herself. "We are," Morgan answered. "We're just waiting for a few more people. Hey, do you think you could help with something while we wait?"

When Zak nodded, Morgan handed him the cards she was holding. "How about you hand these out to the others, and then you can have everybody choose a marker from that bucket over there."

The boy ran off to complete his task and Morgan scanned the room. The other few children were playing with the buckets of toys and Ella and Bo should be arriving any minute.

As if she'd conjured them, the door opened and Ella ran into the room, gave Morgan a quick hug, and then to her surprise, joined the other children on the rug with Bo following closely behind. He was wearing well-worn jeans that hugged his hips in all the right places and a t-shirt, snug on his chest and biceps. He had a heavy sweater slung over his arm.

Morgan swallowed hard against the desire that rose up unexpectedly. Ever since their shared dinner, she'd had trouble keeping Bo out of her thoughts and those thoughts almost always involved what it would feel like to be pressed up against that chest, held tightly by those arms.

"Good afternoon," Bo said, as he came up beside her.

"Hi."

"She's not so shy, is she?" He pointed to Ella, who had plopped herself right in the middle of the other children.

Morgan laughed. "She's really been coming out of her shell with the other kids. I think it's really benefiting her to be here."

A look she couldn't read flashed across Bo's face. "You think so? You really think it's good for her to be at the Lodge?"

There was so much more meaning loaded into Bo's questions, and Morgan knew it. But she didn't know how to respond. After a moment, she looked him square in the eyes, and said, "I think it's good for Ella to be a kid and to have fun."

They stared at each other for a minute, and Bo looked as if he wanted to say something else. Finally, he pointed to the group of children again and asked, "What are those cards that they have?"

Morgan straightened and braced herself for Bo's response. "As you know," she started, "this hiking thing isn't my specialty, but I wanted to offer something to today as well. So I thought it would be fun to do a scavenger hunt."

She waited for Bo to laugh or tell her she was silly.

"I think that's an awesome idea," he said. Morgan turned to look at him. His eyes weren't mocking her. He wasn't laughing. Instead, he looked genuine. Maybe it was a good idea. "Kids can be a tricky group," he said. "Some will love being outside and just enjoying everything that nature has to offer. But others tend to get bored. They have trouble relaxing and need something to keep their minds busy to keep focused. A scavenger hunt is perfect. I'm sure they'll enjoy it."

Morgan beamed. "I was worried."

"I can see that," he said softly. Bo's face turned serious and he took her hand in his. "I promise I won't let anything happen to—"

"Miss Morgan?" Zak squeezed himself in the gap between them and thrust the unused cards at her. "I handed them all out."

She dropped Bo's hand and took a step back. "Good," she said. "I think we're all set then. Ready, Bo?"

"I've never been more ready."

By the time they turned on to the trail that would lead them back to the Lodge, Morgan was ready to laugh at herself. The afternoon hike had gone better than she ever could have expected and she'd been so busy that she hadn't even thought about any of the things in the woods that terrified her. Together with Lisa, she'd helped the kids find everything on the scavenger hunt cards while Bo led them through the trails, pointing things out along the way.

It surprised her to see how someone who claimed to need help learning how to be a dad could be so natural with the children. Maybe it was just being outside that gave him confidence around the kids? He was definitely in his element, and Morgan loved watching him. And she loved watching how Ella, for the most part, stayed closer to Bo than to her. That was definitely progress.

"What do you think, Morgan?"

She shook her head, embarrassed to be caught daydreaming, Morgan looked to her right and to Lisa, who was waiting for an answer to the question she hadn't heard.

"I think——"

"That you weren't listening." Lisa laughed. "You okay? I know this whole nature hike has really thrown you for a loop and all..."

"I'm fine," Morgan said. She picked at a loose thread on her sweater. "It's been a great day. Thank you for all your help."

"Hey, it's my job." Lisa laughed and Morgan found herself laughing along with her.

She liked Lisa. She was smart and great with the kids, and made her job easier, which meant that Morgan would have more time to focus on lining up some fun activities to do with the kids. She still couldn't believe how quickly she'd changed her mind about the job. It wasn't all that long ago that she was ready to cut and run.

"Now, what were you asking me about?"

"Oh, you mean while you were daydreaming about Bo?"

Morgan stopped short and grabbed the other woman's arm, spinning her around to face her. "I wasn't daydreaming about Bo," she said, careful to keep her voice low.

Lisa raised her eyebrows, but didn't say anything else.

"I wasn't," Morgan insisted. "I have no interest in a relationship or...well, anything. That's not why I'm here."

"I believe you," Lisa said, but the gleam in her eyes said that she definitely did not believe Morgan. "Anyway, I was just saying that we should head to the main fire pit and have a campfire. We could roast hot dogs for the kids for dinner—it would be fun."

"And that is why we pay you the big bucks," Morgan joked, grateful for the change in topic. "Do you want to run ahead and get that organized? I'll tell Bo."

Lisa gave her another knowing look, but thankfully took off to get things ready before she could say anything else.

Morgan looked ahead at the small group of kids that was

clustered around Bo. He was squatting and using a stick to point to something on the ground. He had their complete attention while he spoke—all except Ella, who instead of looking at the item of discussion, was staring at her father. Morgan's heart hurt for the little girl. In all her training at school, the first thing they'd been taught was to not get involved or overly attached to the children they were working with. And it had never before been a problem. Sure, she got close to the kids, but not so close that it would be hard to be professional. But Ella was different. Maybe because it wasn't just Ella. She looked to Bo as he caught her eye and smiled. No, it definitely wasn't just thoughts of Ella that twisted her stomach and kept her up at night.

Chapter Eleven

"DO YOU LIKE IT CRISPY? Or barely cooked?" Bo called to the little boy that was waiting for his hot dog.

"Black," the boy yelled.

Bo stuck the roasting stick deeper into the flames. "As you wish," he said.

This was the fifth hot dog he'd cooked, and the end didn't seem to be near as kids lined up for seconds. "Wasn't this your idea?" he asked Lisa, who was pouring juice into paper cups. "Shouldn't you be doing this, too?"

"I'm busy. Besides, you're doing such a good job." Lisa laughed and turned to mop up a mess.

He scanned the group, his eyes landing on Ella, who was finishing up the last bits of her own dinner. She quickly licked her fingers as ketchup squeezed out from the bun but she wasn't fast enough and some dripped on to her pants. She looked up and met Bo's eyes with a look of concern.

He shrugged and gave her a big smile to let her know it was okay. The pants were brand new, but as he was learning, kids were messy. Good thing there were a lot more clothes where those came from. He'd taken the list Morgan had drawn up for him and ordered some clothes online. The shipment had arrived only the day before, and Ella had been thrilled with her new wardrobe. Bo had just laughed while Ella dug through the pile of jeans, sweaters, and shirts. Females must be born with a love for clothing, he'd decided. He didn't want to think of the other option, which was that Ella had never had so many new things before. Not for the first time, Bo wished that he knew more about Tessa and Ella's background.

"Hey there," Morgan said, disrupting his thoughts. It was a welcome interruption. "That looks pretty good." She pointed to the hot dog that was now completely black.

"He's crazy," Bo said as he slid the wiener into a bun and handed it to the eagerly waiting boy. "Me, I like them a little less like charcoal. Have you eaten?"

Morgan waved her hand. "Oh, no. I've been busy."

"There's time to cook one right now."

"It looks as if you have a line." Morgan pointed to the group of kids.

"Oh," Bo said. "I didn't mean that I'd cook you one." He flashed her a grin. "You must have roasted a hot dog before?"

"Um…"

She blushed and Bo felt his body react in what was becoming a familiar way. Damn, but she was beautiful. Especially when she was off guard.

"Well, because you're so outdoorsy now," Bo said, "I'll show you how. It's easy."

Before she could protest, he stuck a raw wiener on a stick for her and prepared his own as well. "Why don't you guys go see if Miss Lisa has some chips or something?" he suggested to the kids. He didn't have to ask twice, and the kids were off running.

"Wow," Morgan said. "If I didn't know better, I'd think that you were an expert with how to handle kids."

"Well, I may not have a lot of experience," he handed her

the stick, "but I do know that no child can resist the allure of potato chips."

She laughed and it was the best sound he'd heard all day because she was so relaxed and at ease with him. It had been great to see her in the woods today. She was so far out of her comfort zone, yet so determined to learn and enjoy it. And from what he'd seen, she had. Bo liked to think that he'd had even a little bit to do with that enjoyment.

"Okay," Bo said. "I'll give you a crash course in weenie roasting. First," he waved his stick in the air, "you stick it in the fire." He stuck his roasting stick into the flames and looked expectantly at Morgan.

She raised her eyebrows at him but followed his lead.

"Great," he said. "Now you wait. And…that's it."

"That's it?"

"You expected more? It's a hot dog, not filet mignon."

Morgan laughed again and they fell into easy silence, both watching the flames licking at the logs. Occasionally, Bo would turn his hot dog, and Morgan would follow his lead. By the time they were done cooking, the kids had grown tired of waiting for seconds and had followed Lisa a few feet away to a grassy, open space where she was leading them in games.

It may have been the company, but Bo couldn't remember ever tasting a better hot dog. He snuck a look over at Morgan, who had also devoured hers. "Good, right?" he asked.

"So good." Morgan licked a stray drop of ketchup off her finger. The innocent action filled him with an intense longing to be on the receiving end of her mouth. He had to stop. Lusting after Ella's teacher, or caregiver, or whatever she was, was not even a little bit appropriate. Especially considering his focus had to be on Ella. At least until he decided on a plan. He owed her at least that much.

"I had fun today," Morgan said. "Thank you for doing this."

He risked another glance towards her. Fortunately for Bo, her hands were clasped together in her lap and nowhere near her mouth. "You were great, a total natural. Oh," he added. "I forgot to tell you how much I liked your hiking boots." He pointed to her feet. "I thought you said you'd never been hiking before."

She blushed a little and ran a hand through her hair. "I haven't. These were a gift. Otherwise, I might have been out there in sneakers or worse."

"Sneakers?"

She nodded. "It's true. I was that unprepared. But my friend Andi gave me these. She's actually the one who told me how amazing it was up here. As you can tell, I don't usually venture very far from the city limits. If it wasn't for her, I probably wouldn't be here at all. Thank goodness for friends."

"Yes," Bo agreed with a smile. "Thank goodness for friends."

"Thanks for the hike, Miss Morgan." Zak wrapped his arms around Morgan and squeezed tightly while Bo watched from the side of the Cub's Club room. It amazed him how good she was with the kids, and how much they loved her.

"I'm glad you had fun, buddy," Morgan said. "I'll see you tomorrow." She waved Zak and his parents out the door and then it was just the three of them. Lisa had left after the hot dog roast, her shift done for the day, and Zak was the last child to be picked up.

"I guess it's time to go," Morgan said, walking toward him. "You didn't have to stay."

"Didn't I?" Bo pointed to Ella, who was fast asleep on the cushions under the treehouse, her clay "horse" in hand. "She looks pretty comfortable. I wouldn't want to be responsible for ruining what looks like a perfectly good nap."

"True, but we're going to have to wake her up." Morgan shrugged apologetically. "I have to lock up for the day."

Bo looked again at Ella and took a few steps in her direction. She'd had such a big day hiking through the woods, she needed her rest. All the kids had enjoyed themselves, but it was Ella who stuck close to him all day, hanging on his every word and pointing at plants. She still wouldn't say much to him, but the fact that she'd enjoyed the time with him outdoors spoke volumes to Bo. He probably shouldn't be thinking too much about his future as a father, at least not until something was decided, but he couldn't help it. He wanted to take her on another hike. Maybe a longer one next time. And maybe—he glanced over at Morgan who was stacking books on the shelf— Morgan would come, too.

"Well?" Morgan asked, coming to stand next to him. "Do you think we can wake her?"

"No," Bo said, "but I'll carry her. Maybe I don't have to disturb her at all." He bent down and slid his arms under her. With a quick motion, he lifted her easily, surprised at how little she weighed. Ella stirred a little and snuggled into Bo's chest. The feeling was foreign, but nice. In the short time Ella had been with him, she hadn't hugged him. Surely she would have had hugs from her mother? How long had it been since she'd had cuddles from someone who loved her? He had no way of knowing and the thought made him sad. He pulled her closer and wrapped his arms around her.

"Bo?"

He jerked his head up. Morgan was watching him with a small smile. He tried to return her smile, but instead his gaze was brought back to Ella. He bent his head and inhaled her fresh little girl scent, mingled with the earthy smells from outside. She was perfect. And the mere thought took his breath away.

"Are you ready, Bo?"

He nodded and as carefully as he could with her in his arms, got to his feet.

Together, they walked down the hall of the Lodge in silence. Bo managed to quit looking at Ella long enough to focus on where he was going. When they reached the main lobby, Bo paused. "I guess I should get her to bed," he said.

A look of disappointment flashed across Morgan's face. But as quickly as it appeared, it was gone. "She's had a pretty big day for such a little girl," she said. "You're going to have to take her out again, she really seemed to take to it. Must be in her blood."

"I don't —"

He'd been about to say that he didn't know where the love for outdoors came from, when he realized that Morgan had been talking about him. He was her father. He looked down at the sleeping child again. It still didn't feel real.

He looked up. "I guess maybe it does. I was thinking earlier how much she liked the hike. Do you know it was the first time she actually seemed to want to be with me? I mean, she doesn't run away from me or anything, but…"

"She doesn't know you," Morgan finished for him.

"No. She doesn't. But she doesn't know you either."

"It's only because I'm a woman," Morgan said. "Like I said before, I think I probably remind her of her mom. It's hard to know why she trusts me. But it's a good thing."

Bo nodded and shifted Ella's weight in his arms. "It is a good thing. I'm so grateful that you stayed. I don't know where I'd—"

"Hey there, buddy." Jeff came up behind Bo and slapped his shoulder in greeting. "I've been looking everywhere for-"

"Jeff!"

Bo absorbed the jostle, but it wasn't enough to keep Ella's eyelids from fluttering open.

"Dammit, Jeff," Bo muttered under his breath.

"Oh, man. I'm sorry." His eyes widened when he saw Ella in Bo's arms. "I didn't know."

Ella stared up at Bo, but she didn't pull away from his chest. The fact that she stayed so close, even when awake, made him inexplicably happy.

"It's fine," Bo said without looking at Jeff. "Did you have a good nap, Ella?"

Ella nodded and stuck her thumb in her mouth.

"I'll get you to bed soon, okay, kiddo?"

She nodded again.

"It's been a big day," Morgan said, by way of explanation.

"Ah," Jeff said with a nod. "By the way, hi, Morgan." Jeff waved his hand sheepishly. "I'm really not usually so rude."

"Yes, he is." Bo shifted Ella so she could see what was going on.

"Hey," Jeff said, turning to Bo, "I really am sorry. I was just so excited to find you."

"Why? What's up?"

"It's overnighter time," Jeff said excitedly. "We have our first booking for tomorrow night. A small group, just a couple and their teenage daughter. I was telling them about Stanley's Cabin, and they thought it sounded great. We leave in the morning."

A million thoughts flashed through Bo's head. An overnight excursion meant good money and that didn't even include the tips. Plus, he was itching to get up on the mountain; it had been too long since he'd been surrounded by nothing but the wild. But a small sneeze, and the growing ache in his arms, gave Bo a whole new type of awareness. Ella. He had more than just himself to consider now. He couldn't leave Ella behind. Besides, who would he leave her with?

Bo's eyes flicked to Morgan. Of course.

Before he could say anything, Morgan beat him to it. "It's a trip with horses?" she asked Jeff, who nodded. "So you take people on a horseback ride into the mountains? Overnight?"

"That's about it," Jeff said. His eyes gleamed. He lived for the overnight trips as well, the chance to take the horses out for a really good trek. He was like a little kid who'd been given a pass to an amusement park. "It's great. Out there with nothing but the wilderness surrounding you. The quiet is so intense that it's almost a religious experience. You'd love it, Morgan."

Bo swallowed a laugh. The idea of Morgan, who until today, had never even been on a hike, participating in an overnight trek was pretty funny.

"What?" Morgan turned to face him, her hands on her hips. "Is something funny?"

Bo bent down to put Ella, who was now completely awake and listening intently, on her feet. He took a moment to regain his composure before standing. "It's just that you're not so much of an outdoorsy type of girl. An overnight trip might be a little much."

"I wasn't saying I wanted to go," Morgan said. She was trying to look put out, but he could see the smile in her eyes. "But," she said, "I bet I can think of someone who would want to go." Morgan looked pointedly down at Ella.

He followed her gaze and sure enough, Ella was looking up with a wide grin on her face. He raised his eyebrow in question and Ella held up her ever-present clay "horse". Of course. Horses.

"Oh," Bo said. He looked to Jeff for help. "I don't know... it's a pretty big trip."

Ella's face fell.

"Are you sure?" Morgan asked. "Ella did such a good job hiking today, and the horses...I'm sure it would be fine."

"I don't-"

"It's a great idea," Jeff jumped in. "It's the perfect time to take her out, Bo. The MacDonalds are a great family, and because it's just a small group, it shouldn't be a problem."

Bo looked at his partner, still unsure. "It would be okay with the MacDonalds?"

"I'll run it past them, but I know they'll be cool with it. The only thing is…" Jeff drifted off, his eyes flicking between Morgan, Bo and then Ella.

"Oh," Bo said, picking up on what Jeff was thinking. "That's a good point."

"What?" Morgan asked warily. "He didn't say anything."

Bo looked at Morgan and gave her the most charming smile he could muster. "It's just that—we might need a little help."

"Help?" She looked between them and Bo saw in her eyes the exact moment that she realized what he was asking.

"Oh no." She held her hands up to defend against the request. "You said yourself I wasn't the outdoorsy type."

"You're a natural," Bo said, before lowering his voice and adding, "I don't think I can do it alone." It was a risk, being so vulnerable, but Ella had really enjoyed the hike earlier and she was clearly excited by the idea.

As if he'd planned it, Ella grabbed Morgan's hand and asked in her tiny voice, "Please?"

Chapter Twelve

MORGAN DIDN'T KNOW the first thing about camping or trail rides, let alone combining the two. For the hundredth time that morning, she wondered how on earth she'd been talked into going on the trip to Stanley's Cabin. It was Ella. She couldn't say no to those sad eyes. And even if she could have said no, it would have meant that Ella wouldn't have been able to go and Morgan refused to be responsible for that disappointment. Even if it meant that she'd have to go way out of her comfort zone. Besides, she wasn't going to deny the fact that spending all that time with Bo wouldn't be a draw as well.

"What else do I need?" Morgan asked Astrid, who was sitting at their kitchen table with a variety of yarn and fabric and was making what looked to be like a half-finished miniature bag in front of her.

"Did you pack the stone I gave you?" Astrid didn't look up as she began to expertly weave a piece of fabric onto the bag.

"I can't take a rock into the woods—there are tons of rocks out there."

"It's not a rock. It's a stone."

Morgan sighed and picked up the crystal from where she'd

tossed it on the bed. "Fine. I'll take it." She tucked it into the outside pocket of her backpack. "But seriously, what am I really going to need out there?"

Astrid turned around, a smile on her face. "Trust me. You'll be glad you have it. The powers of sunstone are strong. It will keep you safe."

"It is pretty," Morgan admitted. "But I'm pretty sure it won't do me any good. Besides, do I need protecting?"

She'd been trying not to think about all the dangers that were waiting for her in the forest. Let alone the fact that they were taking a small child into that danger zone.

Astrid laughed, and abandoning her craft project on the table, she moved to investigate the contents of Morgan's backpack. "You have extra clothes. That's good," she said as she peered inside. "Four extra pairs of socks?" Astrid gave Morgan a questioning look but Morgan only shrugged.

"I hate wet feet."

"It's not calling for rain."

"Bo said there might be snow up high."

Astrid shook her head and continued digging. "You won't need this." She pulled Morgan's make-up kit out of the sack. "In fact, I'd wash your face right now before you go. You don't want to wake up all smeary."

"Smeary?"

"Morgan, there's no running water at the cabin. There is actually a small, although very cold, glacier-fed lake, however."

Bo had told her roughly what to expect from the trip, but there was a part of Morgan that was hoping he'd been kidding. She didn't even want to think about the bathroom situation. Sometimes she was embarrassed by her naiveté when it came to anything outdoors. But she was still willing to try.

Morgan grabbed her make-up kit out of Astrid's hand and went to the bathroom to wash her face. She really was trying and even though Morgan kept telling herself she was just trying to do a good job as a Cub's Club counselor and make a difference for Ella, she couldn't keep lying to herself. It was a whole lot more than that.

She swiped a cotton pad over her eye and blinked at her reflection. Yes, it was a lot more. And the tightening in her stomach confirmed that it was definitely not just about Ella anymore.

———

The stables were located about five miles down the road from the main Lodge building. Known simply as the Ranch, the site consisted of a few outbuildings, surrounded by the main circular building that reminded Morgan of a wagon wheel. From what she was told, it was that building that served as the staging area for all excursions. The upscale log building theme from Castle Mountain Lodge was carried over at the Ranch, and while the place looked rustic and very Western, it still had an underlying feeling of luxury to it.

Morgan pulled the heavy pine door open and called out in the open space, "Hello?"

She checked her watch. She was right on time; everybody must be around somewhere.

Dropping her pack, she walked across the empty room to the floor-to-ceiling windows that covered the far side of the "wagon wheel." The view was breathtaking. Large fenced pastures that had just come to life after a long winter were spread out before her. Horses grazed on the new grass sprouting in the fields and there was Ella standing on the lower rung of a fence, her hand outstretched to a dappled mare that had wandered close. Morgan's breath caught when she saw her. Her first instinct was to run out and pull Ella off the fence, but something told her the child wasn't in danger. Instead, she watched as the horse came near and sniffed Ella's hand. Ella reached out and without a trace of shyness, patted the horse's nose.

Morgan released the breath she'd been holding. Ella was fine. The protectiveness over the little girl surprised her but it shouldn't have. After all, Morgan had always been drawn to kids. Isn't that why she'd chosen to major in child development? All she'd ever wanted was to work with kids and make a difference in their lives. For years, when she thought about her future, that was what she pictured. That, and her own babies in her arms. The familiar pain in her chest sparked to life at the thought that she'd no longer have that. Motherhood wasn't in her future. Her brain knew that; now she just had to make her heart understand.

"Hello?"

Morgan turned around, saved from her own thoughts by the arrival of the MacDonald family.

"Hi there." Morgan pasted a smile on her face and walked toward them, hand outstretched.

"I'm Dan." He took her hand in a firm handshake. "You must be Morgan," he said. "Jeff told us you'd be joining us."

"I hope that's okay. It was all very last minute."

"Don't be silly," the older woman spoke up. Her eyes sparkled with kindness and Morgan instantly warmed to them. "I'm Georgia, and this is our daughter Sawyer."

Sawyer looked to be about fifteen, and much to Morgan's relief, did not seem to be the sulky teenage type. She gave Morgan a wave in greeting before a movement from the barn caught her eye. Morgan looked outside just in time to see Bo and Jeff leading the horses out into the yard. Morgan honed in on Bo. Watching him without being seen was a luxury she didn't even know she wanted. He moved with such ease and handled the horses with such expertise that she couldn't help but be impressed.

"Looks like they're ready," Dan said. "I can't wait to get out there."

They all went out to the yard where Jeff and Bo immediately started to load the gear on the back of the saddles. Morgan took Sawyer, and went to say hello to Ella.

"Sawyer, this is Ella."

The teenager bent down, so she was at Ella's eye level and said, "Hi, Ella. I'm really excited about our trip. Are you?"

Ella blinked slowly and nodded her head, but didn't answer. Sawyer looked up to Morgan for explanation.

"Sometimes Ella doesn't like to talk," Morgan said. "But we're working on it, aren't we Ella?" Morgan looked at her pointedly and waited for her answer.

"Yes," Ella said after a moment.

"Well, I'm glad you're coming, Ella," Sawyer said. She leaned in a little and said, "I don't think I could handle being surrounded by so many adults."

Ella's face split into a smile and she willingly took Sawyer's hand.

"Hey, ladies," Bo called. "Are you ready to go?"

Morgan turned around and her breath caught. His soft, work-worn jeans hugged his thighs; a red plaid shirt peeked out from a denim jacket; and atop his head sat a cowboy hat. Morgan smiled. She hadn't taken him for the cowboy type, but she had to admit, it suited him just fine. Just fine indeed.

Chapter Thirteen

TWO HOURS into the ride and everything was going well. Bo had Ella tucked in front of him on the saddle and because she was so tiny, she fit perfectly. Ella hadn't even hesitated when he told her it was time to climb onto the horse. He'd expected her to be a little frightened, maybe even a bit intimidated by the large stallion, but she'd only held out her arms and allowed Jeff to lift her up. From the moment she sat in the saddle, she had one hand tightly wound in the mane, and with the other, she continually rubbed his neck. Bo thought Ella might be talking to the horse, but every time he looked, he couldn't be sure.

"You still doing okay?" he asked her.

Ella's head whipped around to show Bo a huge smile. Her grin was beautiful and lit up her entire face.

"He's a pretty good guy, isn't he?" Bo said and gave his horse a pat. "He sure likes to get out," Bo said. "But you know what he really likes?"

Ella shook her head.

"He really likes to trot." When Ella looked confused, he added, "That's kind of like running for a horse. Maybe more like a jog. Do you think you'd like to try that with him?"

Her eyes widened in response and she nodded her head so hard that Bo was afraid she'd lose her balance. "Okay," he said with a laugh. "We'll give it a try when we get to the meadow. Now why don't you tell him what our plan is?" He gestured to the horses ears and Ella smiled again before leaning down to whisper something into his ear.

Bringing Ella on the trip had been a good idea. Anything that could make a sad little girl so happy had to be a good idea, and more and more Bo was realizing just how good it felt to make her smile. Bo snuck a glance to his right and to Morgan, who was moving up and down in rhythm with her mare. For such a city girl, she looked like a natural on a horse. Not to mention, incredibly sexy. He watched her tip her head up to the sun, warming her face. She was completely unaware of him watching her, at least he thought she was, but when she turned and aimed her smile at him, he had to laugh.

"You caught me," he said as he rode up along side her. "I just wanted to make sure you were doing okay, but you seem to be handling yourself on Chestnut here pretty well."

Morgan bent forward and stroked the mare's neck. "She's beautiful," she said, "and a perfect traveling companion. She knows she's in control but she hasn't pulled on the reins once."

He tipped his head and examined her. "She is a good horse," Bo said. Morgan's body rolled with the movement of the horse. She wasn't rigid, or tense. Not at all the way he'd expected a city girl to behave on a horse. "Wait a minute," he said. "This isn't your first time on a horse, is it?"

She laughed and gave him a quick smile before shaking her head. "Growing up, my uncle had horses."

"Really? In the city?"

"Come on," she said with a smile. "I may be a city girl, but I did leave sometimes."

He gave her a sidelong look.

"Okay, he had an acreage right on the edge of town. It was

practically the city," she relented. "And really, I haven't been in the saddle for years. But when I was younger, he taught me to jump."

"Jump?"

"Don't look so surprised," she said. "There's a lot you don't know about me."

It was true. There was a lot he didn't know about her. But what he did know, he liked. And despite his vow to avoid distractions, he was drawn to her in a way that was increasingly difficult to ignore.

"Everyone seems to be having a good time," Morgan said, breaking his train of thought. "Especially this one." She pointed in front of Bo's saddle. "Are you having fun, Ella?"

Ella looked up and smiled at Morgan. "Yes," she said quietly. It still boggled Bo how Ella didn't seem to have any trouble speaking to Morgan, but she would only talk to him when absolutely necessary. But their easy silence didn't bother him as much as it had at the beginning. They seemed to be developing an easy way of communicating.

"What's the horse's name, Ella?"

Ella glanced up at Bo quickly before answering, "Horace."

"Horace?"

Ella nodded and returned her attention back to the horse, whispering something else into his ear.

Morgan looked at Bo as if he'd lost his mind. "You named your horse Horace?"

"Technically," Bo said, "he's not my horse."

"But you ride a horse named Horace?"

"I do." He met her gaze, and tried his best to look serious. He failed and together they burst into laughter.

Horace jerked his head and snorted as if he knew they were talking about him, which only made them laugh harder.

After a moment, the laughter faded and Morgan asked, "I just noticed, where's Ella's clay "horse"?"

Bo smiled as he remembered how he'd persuaded Ella to tuck the horse into the pack. "I told her she'd need both hands to hang on to Horace."

"Looks like you were right."

"But don't worry, we brought it. He's wrapped in the pack. I don't know much, but I do know enough not to mess with a woman whose made up her mind about something."

Morgan raised an eyebrow. "Well, I think the real thing is better, anyway. Don't you, Ella?"

Ella nodded, but didn't look up.

"I'm glad she likes it so much," Morgan said. "And I think she's a natural like her daddy."

Daddy.

The word slammed into him and sent his thoughts spiraling. Intellectually, Bo knew he was Ella's father. But it was still new. Too new. Daddy. He still wasn't convinced that he could be someone's daddy. There was a lot of responsibility. Maybe too much. But the more he rolled the word around in his head, the better it felt. He looked down at the little blond head that was bobbing along with the motion of the horse and instinctively bent and dropped a kiss on the top of it.

By the time they got to Lake of the Hanging Glacier and the cabin, it was late afternoon and everyone, including Ella, was more than ready to get off their horses.

Bo left Jeff to brush out the horses with some help from the MacDonald family, who enjoyed being as hands-on as possible with the animals. They felt it gave them the entire experience, and Bo wasn't complaining because it gave him a few minutes to escape and check on Ella and Morgan. The moment they dismounted, Ella was off exploring, which meant that Morgan was right behind her. And more than anything else, those were the two people that Bo wanted to spend time with.

Just the realization of that shocked him. He'd never in his life wanted to spend time with a woman longer than one night, and Morgan, who he'd never even kissed, captivated him in a way he could neither explain, nor control. The thought was frightening, but instead of spending too much time thinking about it, Bo headed towards the cabin, and the field that lay beyond it.

Even though Bo would have liked to skip his duties completely, he still had a job to do. And there were going to be some hungry people if he didn't get dinner started. Bo unlocked the simple padlock that held the door closed and went inside. The cabin was simple, and far from the luxury of the Lodge. But considering the fact that it was located in the middle of nowhere, it was pretty nice. It consisted only of a simple room with a table and chairs and three small bedrooms that led off the main room. The space was cozy, but you didn't spend all day on a horse to hang out inside Stanley's Cabin. The real treat was outside.

Bo pulled the curtains back and pushed up the window to let the cool spring air in. The mountain meadow lay out before him. Fresh with new growth, it was a carpet of green dotted by the first wildflowers of the season. The lake with the glacier, still full of ice and snow, lay just beyond. And there was Ella, her hand already full of blooms. She ran, her hair flying out behind her as Morgan chased her in what looked like a game of tag.

He could have watched them all day, but he had to get things started. He moved to the wood stove that also acted as the furnace; after a few minutes a fire sparked to life and he started reheating the chili that he'd had the Lodge chef pack. Experience taught him that the guests were always hungry after a long day on horseback, so he had the kitchen staff prepare a hearty chili that they could enjoy with a loaf of fresh bread.

Dinner was simmering, and Bo was slicing the loaf when Jeff came in the door, carrying both of their packs and Morgan's, too. "Smells good in here," he said, on his way through the room to the back bedroom. When he reappeared, he sank heavily into one of the chairs. "The MacDonalds are soaking in a bit of nature. They decided to hike down to the falls. They should be back in thirty."

"Sounds good," Bo said. He tasted the chili. "Dinner will be ready when they are."

Jeff stretched his arms over his head, relaxing into the chair. "Great ride out there today, wasn't it?"

Jeff loved nothing more than getting out on the horses, unless of course it was riding deep into the wilderness on the horses. And Stanley's Cabin was about as remote as it got.

Bo smiled and tossed his friend the heel of the loaf. "It was a good ride. Ella loved it," he said. "I was worried, but she handled it like a pro."

"She wasn't the only one who handled it well," Jeff said with a wink.

"Who, Morgan?" Bo asked. "I didn't notice."

Jeff shot him a look to let him know he wasn't buying it for a minute. "Right," he said. "All you've been doing is noticing. You got it bad for her. I've never seen you look at a woman like that."

Bo turned away from the stove. He was pretty sure he'd regret asking, but he did anyway. "Like what?"

"Like you can't get enough. Like everything she does and says is perfect," Jeff said. "Like you love her."

Love? Bo's thoughts spiraled through his head, crashing into one another. He couldn't process what Jeff had said. Hell, he couldn't even process what he was feeling. But Jeff was wrong. He had to be. Bo didn't love anyone. Never had. But Morgan...

"What are you talking about?" Bo finally managed to choke out the question.

Jeff raised his eyebrow in response.

"You're wrong," Bo said. Movement outside caught his eye and he found himself watching while Morgan and Ella held their arms out as they spun around in the center of the field.

Jeff followed his friend's gaze and laughed. "Right," he said slowly. "Like your whole world isn't outside that window, right now."

His friend's words hit him hard and he turned in a daze. He wanted to protest again but he knew Jeff was right. And that scared the hell out of him.

Chapter Fourteen

DESPITE BEING SO high up in the mountains, Morgan was surprised at how warm it was. And because it was such a beautiful evening, the group gathered around the large picnic table outside the cabin for dinner. Morgan was impressed with how Jeff and Bo had pulled together such a delicious-looking dinner. She wasn't sure what she'd expected, but it definitely wasn't a nicely set table complete with red checked tablecloth, white dishes, and even a bottle of wine spread out before her. The flowers that Ella had picked earlier completed the setting with the place of honor in the middle of the table.

"It smells amazing, Bo," Georgia said. "Every time we come here, I'm just so amazed at your culinary skills."

Bo laughed. "And I keep telling you, I can't take any responsibility for this. The kitchen staff down at the Lodge does it all. I simply reheat it."

"Well, you reheat very well," Dan said.

They all laughed and passed the food around. Remembering that the MacDonalds were paying guests was difficult for Morgan—they were so friendly and comfortable to be around that the whole group felt as if they were old friends.

Jeff poured the wine, with juice for Ella and a soda for Sawyer, and they toasted to a great ride and the first trek of the season.

"I heard you hiked down to the falls?" Bo asked. "How were they?"

"Gorgeous as always," Georgia said. "I could sit there forever watching the water rush past."

"Water falls?" Morgan looked to Bo, but it was Sawyer that answered.

"Oh, Morgan. You have to go see them," Sawyer said. "They are so cool. Totally worth the hike."

"A hike?" She'd enjoyed the hike she'd taken with the kids, but Morgan was pretty sure that the word hike held a completely different meaning so high in the mountains. "I'm not sure—"

"It's really not too bad," Jeff cut in. "And it is beautiful. Maybe Bo could take you tomorrow."

Jeff smiled and shot Bo a quick look that Morgan didn't miss.

"I'm not sure." Morgan looked between the two of them. "I'm not much of a hiker."

"Morgan, you have to go!" Sawyer practically bounced out of her seat with the enthusiasm of youth. "It's totally not hard. Well, not too hard. And so worth it."

"It is spectacular, Morgan," Dan said.

Morgan looked towards Bo, who still hadn't said anything. "Maybe I should go," she said slowly. "I'm feeling adventurous." And she was, and not just about hiking, which is why she added, "Would you take me, Bo?"

Morgan didn't miss Jeff's satisfied smile before he shoveled another piece of bread in his mouth. A look of shock flashed across Bo's face before dissolving into an easy smile. "Sure," he said. "If you're sure you can handle it."

Her confidence lapsed for a moment but she thought back to the stone Astrid had made her pack. Tucking it into her pocket before they left probably wouldn't be a terrible idea. "I do want to go," Morgan said, trying to sound more self-assured than she felt. "If it's as beautiful as everyone says, I don't want to miss it."

"Then we'll go." His eyes held a question, but for the life of her, she couldn't figure out what it was. Before she had a chance to read too much into it, he looked into his bowl of chili and said, "First thing in the morning, before we head back to the Lodge."

The group fell into easy conversation again while they finished their meal. But Morgan noticed that Bo didn't make eye contact with her again. What was up with him? She'd been pretty sure they'd finally gotten past their rocky start and were actually starting to be friends. But ever since the falls were brought up, Bo would barely even look at her. Maybe she'd been wrong.

"How do you feel about making s'mores, Ella?" Jeff was up and gathering the empty dishes from the table. At the mention of dessert, Ella, who was starting to look very tired, perked up again. "Tell you what," Jeff continued. "Why don't you help me clear this table while the others get the fire started? That way it'll be ready when we are. Sound good?"

Ella nodded and jumped up to help.

"Bribery by way of marshmallow always works," Jeff said with a smile.

Morgan turned to ask Bo whether he needed help with the fire, but when she looked, he was already gone. With a sigh, she pushed up from the table and went to help Jeff with the dishes.

"Ella, you are an amazing chef," Georgia said as she shoved the last bite of a s'more into her mouth.

"That's for sure. But I'm stuffed," Dan said. He rubbed his

stomach in a dramatic show. "I think if I have any more I'm going to burst. And that would be messy."

Ella giggled and Sawyer rolled her eyes.

Morgan smiled and licked her fingers clean of the remaining marshmallow strands that stuck to them. She looked up and caught Bo staring at her but before she could smile at him he jumped up into the shadows. His behavior had only gotten stranger since dinner, but for the life of her, Morgan couldn't figure out what'd caused the shift in his attitude.

Despite the strangeness, the fire had been fun and Morgan couldn't remember the last time she'd ever enjoyed a campfire, if ever. But sitting around the open flames, watching the fire lick at the logs that Jeff and Bo kept piling in had been relaxing and kind of therapeutic in a way. But it was listening to everyone's stories about past expeditions or camping trips that had been the real highlight. Morgan hadn't realized how much she'd been missing by sticking close to the city.

Everyone had a story. Everyone but Bo. He'd been conspicuously absent most of the night. When he wasn't chopping wood, he was stacking it or off getting more. Morgan couldn't shake the feeling that his absence had something to do with her. She just couldn't figure out what it was.

"I think it's probably time for you to go to bed, Ella." Bo reappeared out of the darkness and crouched next to the little girl.

Morgan was ready for Ella to protest or put up a fuss. And if she were any other four-year-old, she might have. But Ella was definitely not any other four year old. She nodded and held her hand out to Bo.

"Would you like me to—"

"No." Bo spoke without looking at Morgan. "I'll go tuck her in and then come back to tend to the fire."

Morgan pushed down the sudden hurt feelings that sprung up. It was nice to see Bo stepping up and being a father to

Ella. And of course, it was so good to see Ella warming up to him. They were figuring each other out, and that was what was supposed to happen. She knew that. And she also knew that it didn't make any sense for her feelings to be so hurt when she wasn't needed. But sometimes knowing it wasn't enough. Morgan looked down at her feet and kicked at a pinecone.

"You know what?" Dan sat up, and held out his hand to his wife. "I think I'm going to hit the sack, too. It's been a long day."

"Sounds good," Georgia said, allowing Dan to pull her to her feet. "Sawyer?"

"Sawyer?"

All heads turned toward the teenager, who was leaning against a large stump, head in her hand, fast asleep.

"So much for the energy of youth," Dan said, laughing. He gently shook his daughter awake and together the family headed into the cabin for the night.

When they were gone, Jeff turned to Morgan and asked, "How about you? Are you ready to call it a night?"

After the long day, she should probably go to bed, especially considering they had another big day ahead of them. But as Morgan looked into the dancing flames of the fire and felt the heat on her face, she wasn't ready for it to end.

"Is it okay if I stay up for bit? Or do you need to put the fire out?"

"Nah," he said. "There's no hurry. It is nice, isn't it? There's nothing I like better than a campfire under the stars. I'm going to go check on the horses and make sure they're settled in for the night. Will you be okay for a few minutes on your own?"

"Of course. Why wouldn't I?"

"Well, you are a city girl," Jeff said as he stood. "And we are pretty far away from civilization."

Morgan threw a pinecone at him and laughed. "I'll be fine. I promise I won't let anything get me."

He caught it easily in one hand and said, "Okay but, if you hear anything you think might be an animal, run for the cabin."

Morgan tried to make out his features across the fire, but they were hidden in the shadows so she couldn't tell whether he was joking or not. "I'm fine," she said after a moment, but even as she said it a sense of unease washed over her.

"Okay, I won't be long."

He disappeared quickly into the dark night and Morgan focused on the fire in front of her. The night air was chilly, but the heat from the flames was almost enough to keep her warm. She pulled her legs up and wrapped her arms around her knees. Something about the way the flames licked at the logs was hypnotizing. The crackle of the sticks and twigs burning pulled her in and she got lost watching the flames dance and move.

The entire day had been so fun and she really couldn't believe that in such a short time she'd gone from a girl who never set foot into the woods to a girl that didn't want to leave them. Andi and Eva wouldn't believe it when she told them.

Morgan chuckled to herself and tipped her head back so she could stare up into the sky that was anything but dark. Even without the glow of a full moon, the sky was bright and popping with the light of millions of stars. She'd never seen anything like it. Even at the Lodge, where she was able to see a lot more stars than she ever had in the city, there was still too much light from the buildings to see the magical starlit world that surrounded her up at the cabin.

She watched a shooting star streak across the sky, and Morgan tried to make a wish but she couldn't decide quickly enough about what to wish for and then the moment passed.

A distant owl calling from the trees and then a loud snap,

like a stick being stepped on, brought Morgan firmly out of her daydreams and directly into the present. She sat up with a jolt and stared across the fire into the darkness, trying to remember what Jeff had said about animals. Should she run or play dead?

He was probably just back from checking the animals already. "Jeff? Is that you?" She tried to sound tough and in charge but her voice came out as little more than a whisper.

No answer.

Her heart pounded in her chest but Morgan couldn't move. She was frozen by the fear of what she couldn't see in the darkness. Her thoughts flew out of control as she tried to remember what she'd heard about wild animals. If it were a bear, she should run. And a cougar...damn, she couldn't remember.

Another noise. A crunch of leaves or grass. Closer this time.

Chapter Fifteen

"DAMN IT," Bo muttered under his breath. He hadn't meant to scare her.

After tucking Ella into her bunk, he'd decided to check the horses, anything to give him some space from Morgan and the feelings he was having. The feelings that scared the hell out of him.

But Jeff was with the horses and he'd already done everything that needed to be done, so he sent Bo to take care of the fire. He failed to mention that Morgan was still up.

Watching her from a distance was a beautiful kind of torture. Sitting on the ground with the warm glow from the fire illuminating her face, Morgan looked completely at peace, and more gorgeous than Bo had seen her yet. He'd leaned up against the wall of the shed and watched her, unseen. Morgan kept surprising him, especially earlier on the horses and her willingness to try everything that was so new to her. She was his opposite in so many ways. It didn't make sense for her to be having such an effect on him.

He probably would have stood there all night watching her if the owl hadn't chosen that moment to call, causing him to startle and step on the stick. The trance broken, Morgan's head jerked up and she called out to Jeff. She was scared; Bo could see it on her face and he instantly felt like an ass. He grabbed an old wool blanket from a shelf in the shed and made his way to her.

"Is anyone there?" Morgan asked. Bo's chest tightened when he heard the fear in her voice.

"It's me," he said softly. He moved into the circle of light cast by the campfire.

"Bo! What the hell are you doing? You scared me half to death!" Her transformation from terrified to angry was instantaneous and almost made him chuckle, but he was smart enough to know that it was never a good idea to laugh at a woman right after he'd scared the daylights out of her.

"I'm sorry," he said instead. "Here." Bo shook out the wool blanket and moved around the fire so he could drape it around her shoulders. "I thought you might be cold."

She took it and pulled it tight. "Thank you." She still looked pissed, but she no longer looked as if she was going to attack him.

Instead of moving back to the other side of the fire, Bo sat on the ground next to her. She was close enough to touch, and he had to fight against the overwhelming urge to reach out and take her hand. Instead, he grabbed a long stick and poked at the fire.

They sat in silence watching the sparks fly when he jabbed the stick into the glowing embers. Finally, it was Bo who said, "I really am sorry that I scared you." He snuck a look over his shoulder. She didn't look at him. Her eyes were fixed on the flames. "I didn't mean to."

"It's fine," she said slowly. "I thought I was alone is all and Jeff had mentioned something about animals. You just caught me off guard." She tossed a twig into the fire. "Are you okay?"

Her question caught him by surprise and he turned to see her looking at him.

"I mean," she continued, "you've been acting kind of strange all night. I was just wondering if you were okay."

He smiled and poked at the fire again. Apparently, his efforts at trying to create distance from Morgan hadn't gone unnoticed. They also hadn't done him any good at all. "I'm fine," he said. "I was just thinking about a few things. This place makes me think is all."

"I could see that," Morgan said after a minute. "It's so beautiful out here. I had no idea." Her voice was filled with emotion, almost as if she might cry. Bo had seen people, even grown men, reduced to tears by the raw beauty of the mountains. It wasn't uncommon. Something about the glacier seemed to bring things out in people—things they weren't even sure they needed to get out. "I've never seen so many stars," Morgan continued. She tipped her head back just as she had earlier, only this time he was close enough to see the smooth skin of her neck as she stretched back. "The sky is so full of them that it's almost white. It makes a person feel pretty small, like there's so much more out there."

If she'd been a guest, or any other visitor to Stanley's Cabin, Bo would have pointed out some of the more common constellations. If he'd been thinking rationally, if he'd been thinking about maintaining a professional distance, that's exactly what he would have done. But she wasn't any other visitor. He didn't know quite what Morgan was to him, but there was something about her that drew him. Something, that despite his best efforts, he couldn't shake. Maybe it was that look in her eyes when she'd thought no one was looking? That same look she had when she was sitting, watching the flames before he'd sat.

He should leave it. He should leave her, get up and put out the fire before it was too late. Despite the mess of feelings he had, he knew he couldn't treat her like she was any other woman because Morgan wasn't like any other woman and he'd never felt so strongly before. Which meant there was no way he could walk away.

He watched her for a moment more as she gazed up at the stars. "Morgan," Bo said, before his rational brain could stop him. "I'm really glad you came with us. It means a lot to me."

It seemed to take forever, but then she sat up, pulling her gaze away from the stars and looked directly at him. Her face was illuminated by the glow of the fire, and Bo could clearly see the uncertainty on her face. "Because of Ella, you mean?"

"No." His voice was rough and throaty to his own ears. "Because of me." He closed the slight gap between them and reached out to brush back a tendril of hair that had come loose from her ponytail. His fingers traced the soft curve of her cheek as he tucked the hair behind her ear. A small puff of air escaped Morgan's lips and she closed her eyes.

Despite everything his brain was telling him, his heart was speaking much louder, so he slid his hand behind her head, wrapping his fingers through her hair and pulling her gently towards him. He leaned over and bridged the small gap between them. When he finally touched her lips with his own, he knew he'd never want to stop. She tasted sweet like marshmallows and something he couldn't define. Her lips yielded to his and slowly he explored her mouth with his while his other hand came to rest on her cheek. He let his thumb gently stroke the soft skin on her face while he lost himself in her.

Bo's gut clenched at the sensations she produced in him. Never had he kissed a woman so softly and had it stir up so much passion. For that matter, never had he experienced such intense feelings with any woman, which was probably because what he was feeling—it wasn't purely physical. That was the part that worried him.

With a slight groan, Bo pulled back to give them air. It took her a second to open her eyes but when she did, the dazed, passion-clouded expression she wore almost made him take her in his arms for the second time.

"I'm—"

"Don't." She cut him off.

Bo nodded and sat back. He let his hand trail down her shoulder as he moved, so it rested on the ground next to her. She was right.

He picked up the poker stick and jabbed it in the coals, stirring up the flames of the fading fire. It sparked to life again, providing an instant heat. The weight of Morgan's hand covering his startled him and he turned. She'd slid one arm from the blanket and was watching him intently. He turned his hand over so hers rested on his palm.

"I shouldn't," he said with a crack in his voice. "There's so much…"

"Ella."

Bo nodded. "Yes, Ella." He closed his fingers over hers, encasing her hand despite his uncertainty. "I don't know what to do." He hadn't thought about his call to Clara Kersey in days and he still hadn't heard from her, but being so close to Morgan stirred up a lot of unanswered questions.

Morgan nodded. "I'm not going to pretend to know what it's like to be surprised with a four-year-old," she said. "I don't know what it's like to have a child at all." Her voice broke, but when Bo looked, her face gave away nothing. "But she's beautiful," she continued, "and with time, you'll figure each other out. It's going to be okay, Bo."

Somehow when she said it, Bo believed it.

He squeezed her hand in his and looked into her eyes. "You know what? I think you might be right."

"You weren't sure?"

Bo reached up and slipped his free hand behind her head so he could wind his fingers through her silky hair. He kissed her once on the lips before pulling back. "Up until very recently I wasn't sure about a lot of things," he said without releasing her.

"And now?"

He pulled her into his arms, letting his kiss answer her question.

Chapter Sixteen

"WATCH YOUR STEP HERE," Bo called back to Morgan, who was doing her best to keep up to him on the trail to the falls. She had to concentrate so she didn't trip over the exposed roots and stones, while Bo seemed to bound over the obstacles without any trouble.

After a quick breakfast, they'd left the rest of the group at the cabin so Bo could take her to the falls as promised. The night before, at the campfire, Morgan had let herself believe that maybe she could act on her feelings for Bo. She hadn't even thought about it when he'd kissed her. And maybe that was the point. It was easy and it felt natural. She didn't have to overthink it.

Morgan stopped walking and looked up. Bo was standing in the middle of the trail, watching her with a secret smile on his face. Her stomach flipped at the sight but she forced herself to focus.

"Are you waiting for me?"

"Of course," he said, and extended his hand for her. She took it and in one smooth move, he pulled her up the rocky trail so they were standing close together. "I was waiting for this." Without letting go of her hand, Bo pulled her tight with his free arm and his lips crushed hers. They were both out of breath when he finally drew back.

Morgan's heart was beating so hard she wasn't sure she'd be able to make it down the rest of the trail and she had to work hard to get her breathing under control again. When they'd finally been able to let each other go the night before, put the fire out, and make their way to their separate beds, she wasn't sure how things would be when they woke up. And around the others earlier that morning, Bo had acted the same as always.

As if he'd read her mind, he kissed her again and said, "I've wanted to do that all morning."

Her heart did a happy dance that surprised even her. Just a few days ago she'd been dead set against starting any kind of relationship with anyone. But there was something about Bo, and standing alone with him in the middle of a mountain path felt like the most natural thing in the world at that moment.

"We should get moving," he said but he didn't move. "I want you to see Forgotten Falls."

"Forgotten Falls? Is that what they're really called?"

He nodded and unwrapped his arms from her but didn't let go of her hand as they started back down the trail.

They walked quietly for a few minutes and when Bo had to let go of Morgan's hand to navigate the trail, it immediately felt empty. He didn't offer any more explanation, but something about the name of the falls resonated with Morgan. The tragically sad name had to have a story behind it. She was about to ask Bo about it when all of a sudden, she could hear the roar of the water.

"Is that it?" she asked, barely containing her excitement. She'd only ever seen Niagara Falls on a family vacation as a child, but had definitely never done anything as outdoorsy as hiking into a waterfall.

"It's just around that bend." Bo pointed and stepped out of the way as Morgan charged ahead. "Be careful," he called after her, but she could hear the laughter in his voice.

Morgan stopped short and stood in wonder at the miracle of nature that stood before her. She wasn't sure anything could be any more beautiful than Lake of the Hanging Glacier and the meadow up at the cabin, until that moment. Just as Bo'd said, the falls were right around the bend. When Morgan turned the corner, she hadn't been prepared to see the water cascading over boulders in a frantic dance down the side of the mountain, crashing twenty feet below to a small, rocky pool. The water drained into a stream that disappeared farther into the trees as it made its way down the mountainside. Morgan walked toward the edge of the pool through a fine mist rising from the water's surface. She clambered over the rocks before turning back to Bo.

"Go ahead," he called to be heard over the roar of the water. "Test the water. But don't fall in."

She gave him a look and turned back. She'd never seen such clear water before. Along the edge, she could see the rocks at the bottom. She could also feel the chill and she knew even before touching it that it was going to be cold. Morgan stuck her fingers in anyway and immediately yanked them back out.

"It's freezing!"

"Of course it is," Bo answered. "That water is coming straight off the glacier. The freshest water you'll ever drink. Better than that fancy bottled stuff, anyway."

She laughed and put her fingers in again, this time waving them through the water, letting her skin absorb the frigid temperature. It only took seconds before they were numb and she pulled them out.

"Come here," Bo said. "Let me warm you up."

Morgan pushed herself up from the rock and carefully made her way back to where Bo was waiting. He took her hand; the warmth of his skin instantly heated her. Bo turned her around so she could watch the water as it crashed down the falls.

"It's beautiful," she said.

Bo pulled her backward so she was leaning into his chest. "You're beautiful," he murmured into her hair.

A thrill went through her at his words, but Morgan was too focused on the sight before her to dwell on it. She let herself become hypnotized by the falling water and the way it swirled in wild currents before easing out into the stream. After a few minutes, Bo led her farther away from the chilly water's edge to a flat rock where they could sit together and still enjoy the view.

Something dug into her leg as she sat and Morgan reached deep into the pocket of her jeans to pull out the small red stone that Astrid had given her.

"What's that?"

Morgan blushed as she slipped the rock through her fingers. "It's just a silly stone that Astrid gave me. She said it would offer me protection."

Bo gently took the rock from her hand. "Sunstone," he said. "She's right. But did she tell you what else sunstone is for?"

Morgan lifted an eyebrow in question. "Please, enlighten me."

"It's been said that sunstone is supposed to promote attraction and sexual energy." He spun the stone in his fingers and winked at her before she snatched the gemstone away.

"Stop it," she said. "You're full of it."

"Am I?" Bo's eyes twinkled with mischief and he reached out for her, easily pulling her close. When he slipped his arm around her, it felt like the most natural thing in the world and

Morgan let herself go with the feeling. And when their lips met in a deep kiss, she silently thanked Astrid for giving her the sunstone, no matter what its actual purpose was for.

When they pulled apart, he took her hand and pulled her to her feet. "Before we go," Morgan said, "will you tell me why they call them Forgotten Falls?"

Bo didn't answer right away but turned her around so her back was once again pressed up against his chest. His hands moved slowly up and down her arms, keeping her warm against the blasting cold water only feet away. "Well, some say it's because the glacier up above is so beautiful that these falls are often forgotten, but I've heard a different story."

"Will you tell me?"

"It was a love story," he said. "Are you sure you want to hear it?"

She turned around in his arms so she could see his face. "Why do I get the feeling that it's not a happy-ever-after love story?"

He offered her a small smile by way of an answer.

"As you guessed, it's not a happy story. But legend has it that there was a young Native girl who was madly in love with a warrior. But before they could be together, the warrior had to go off on a hunt with the other men. He would be gone for months, and the girl was afraid he would forget about her and fall in love with another. The warrior promised his love that he could never forget her heart, and he would come to her at the falls on the third night of his return."

"Did he come back?"

"He did," Bo said. "As planned, the hunting party returned and the girl watched from afar during the festivities and feasts. Then, on the third night, she snuck away and waited here for him to come to her. She waited through the night and into the next day, not giving up hope on her warrior. Finally, after two days, she was worried that something might have happened to him so she made the journey down to the village."

Morgan lifted her head and faced Bo. "And was he okay?"

He nodded. "She found him at the center of a wedding feast, with his new bride."

A chill ran through Morgan, and she reflexively snuggled closer to Bo.

"It turns out that the girl was right," Bo said. "Her warrior—"

"Forgot her heart," Morgan finished. "Forgotten Falls."

She turned to look at the falls again, this time picturing the young girl waiting for her love to come to her, all the while not knowing he was marrying another. Bo was right—it was a sad story. She felt Bo's arm around her, his thumb stroking circles on her shoulder.

"It's a good story," Bo said, "and the tourists like it. But I don't like to think of it being true."

Morgan turned so she could see him. "Me neither," she said. "I'd prefer to think that her warrior came home to her and they lived happily ever after."

Bo laughed. "Do you think it's that easy? Living happily ever after, I mean?"

His question stopped her because even if it wasn't possible, at that moment with his body warming hers and the sunstone smooth in her fingers, for the first time in a long time, Morgan wasn't thinking of the future. She was only thinking of the way it felt to be in Bo's arms with the water crashing against the rocks. And that was all she needed.

Chapter Seventeen

BEING WITH MORGAN WAS EASY. Bo'd never been so comfortable around a woman before but the last few days had been great, never mind the night before when he finally threw out all his stupid excuses and kissed her. Once he'd started, he hadn't wanted to stop and sleeping in the bunk room with her so close, yet totally unreachable had been like some form of torture. But he was smart enough to know that trying to sneak into her bed would have been pushing things way too far, way too fast. Let alone what Ella would have thought about it.

Ella. Just thinking about her brought a smile to his face.

"You look happy," Morgan said. She sat up from where she'd been lounging on the rock next to him. "What are you thinking about?" The stray piece of hair that never seemed to stay put slipped over her forehead and Bo reached up to tuck it away.

"I am happy," he said. "But I was just thinking of Ella. She really seems to like the mountains. I think being here is helping her.""

"I don't think it's just the mountains that are helping."

Morgan slid forward so she was sitting directly in front of him. "Ella's healing and there are a lot of factors involved. This is a very sensitive time in her development."

Bo tilted his head and raised an eyebrow. "Wow," he said. "You seem to know a lot about it and don't get me wrong," he held out his hands to ward off any objection, "I know you work with kids all day, but…"

"It's what I did in a past life."

"Worked with kids?"

"Yes, well, sort of." She ran her hands through her hair, smoothing her ponytail before looking at him again. "I used to work with troubled children, using play therapy methods to help them through traumatic situations."

Bo straightened his spine and looked at her with amazement before remembering the first day at the Cub's Club. "Wait a minute. You were going to leave," he said. "I know most of the kids up here aren't going through any kind of trauma in their lives, but why would you take this job just to leave right away?"

Morgan looked down at her boots before answering. "I didn't actually want to work in my field. I was supposed to have a job planning events."

"What? Why?" He searched her face for a clue to what she was talking about. Morgan was without a doubt one of the most intriguing, if not confusing, women he'd ever met.

"I don't like to talk about it."

She looked so sad at that moment that Bo wanted to pull her into his arms and tell her that it didn't matter what her reasons were. But she also looked like a woman who, despite her protests, *did* need to talk about it.

"You can tell me," he said, "I mean, if you want to."

"It's just…" she drifted off but he waited. Soon she continued, "Have you ever had things all planned out the way you think they're going to go and then something happens to change everything?"

He raised an eyebrow in response. "Um...yeah, I do kinda know what that feels like."

She burst out laughing as she realized what she'd said. "Oh, Bo, I'm sorry. I totally forgot. Of course you know."

"It's okay," he said, trying not to laugh. "I'm still trying to get used to it myself."

Her outburst lightened the mood and she was much more relaxed when she started talking again. "I wanted to work with kids. Like I said, it's all I ever wanted to do. But I also wanted children of my own," she said. "I mean, ever since I was a kid myself. I used to dream about being a mother."

"Used to?"

Her eyes filled with tears and Bo's instinct was to lean over and kiss them away.

"That's the thing." She looked away and swiped at her eyes before looking back. "I don't know why I'm telling you this but not too long ago I found out that I won't be able to have children. Ever. That's why I came here. I wanted to get away from kids and start fresh. Somewhere where I didn't have to think about it all the time."

"And then you got pushed into working at the Cub's Club and with Ella," Bo said. He wiped a tear from her cheek and took her hand in his. "Thank you for that. I really mean it."

Morgan squeezed her hand and managed a small smile. "I'm glad I stayed."

"You are?"

"I am, and as far as Ella goes," she said. "It's not just the mountains that are helping her heal. It's you."

"What do you mean—me?"

Morgan reached out and took his other hand. Her fingers were a little cold from being near the water, but her touch sent a heat through him to his core. "She's bonding with you,"

Morgan said. "I think she's finally starting to feel safe with you, like you'll protect her and care for her."

"Of course I will."

"But she didn't know that when she first came," Morgan said quickly. "Think about it, Bo. Ella lost the only parent she ever knew. The one she thought would take care of her. And then she was just given to you without any warning. Children who've been through something like that have to learn all over again how to trust. They need an opportunity to bond with their new caregiver."

He let her words sink in.

"You think she likes me?"

Morgan laughed. "Yes. She likes you. Is that so hard to believe?" She dropped his hands and pushed off the ground. "I'm going to fill my water bottle with some of this amazing glacier water you've been raving about."

Bo thought about her question, trying to wrap his head around it. Morgan may have always wanted to be a mother, but he'd never given any thought to being a father. Not until it all changed. He watched as Morgan knelt at the edge of the water. Just about a month ago, he'd still been a single man ready for a fun summer of leading treks in the woods and no-strings-attached sex. He never would have imagined that he'd be sitting here with a woman that made his heart beat fast and his blood run hot, thinking about a future that could very possibly include her. And his daughter.

By the time they got back to the cabin, everyone had finished exploring around the glacier and they were ready to hit the trail. After getting everyone organized on their horses, Bo hoisted Ella on the saddle and they headed down the trail with Jeff bringing up the rear.

Bo was enjoying the peace, and the opportunity to think about what had happened at the falls. He was lost in thought when Jeff rode up alongside of him on the trail. "Hey, buddy," he said, when he got close. One look at his friend's face and there was no secret what Jeff was going to want to talk about.

"It was a good trip," Bo said. "And for the first one of the season, I—"

"What's going on with Morgan?"

Bo looked again at his friend, whose grin told him that Jeff knew exactly what was going on. He glanced behind him to see Morgan, riding next to Georgia, deep in conversation about something. She smiled when she caught him looking at her and a warmth flooded him.

"It's like that, is it?" Jeff laughed when Bo turned around again. Bo knew his feelings for Morgan were written all over his face so instead of answering his friend, he shrugged and smiled at the memory of Morgan's kiss.

"I never thought I'd see the day when someone would tame you," Jeff said. "But it's about time."

Bo shot him a look. "Nobody said anything about being tamed." Even as he said the words, Bo knew Jeff wasn't going to believe it. Heck, he didn't believe it himself.

"Whatever you say, man." Jeff rolled his eyes. "But whatever you do, don't screw it up," he added, and pointed to Ella who had resumed her position half holding on, half hugging Horace. "Because I think someone else really likes Morgan, too."

"Of course she does," Bo said. "And of course I'm not going to screw it up."

"Look, all I'm saying is that it's not just you that you need to worry about anymore," Jeff said. "It can't be about just having a good time. Because if you sleep with her and then get ready to move on to the next one—"

"Hey. I told you, it's not like that."

"Whatever you say, man." Jeff held up one hand in mock defense. "But I have to tell you, before I went in to foster care, my mom…well, let's just say that she didn't have the best track record with men." Bo watched Jeff's face cloud over with the memories. "It was hard, man. Just when I started getting attached to a guy and thought maybe he'd be my dad, he was gone and there was someone new. It messes with a kid, ya know?"

"I didn't know," Bo said. "I'm sorry that happened to you, buddy."

Jeff waved his hand in the air. "Don't worry about it. It was a long time ago. I'm just thinking about this little one here." He pointed down to Ella, who was still entranced by the horse. "It looks like you guys are starting to find your groove and I don't want to see you do anything that will screw it up."

Bo glanced back again and said, "Really, it's not like that with Morgan."

"Well, whatever it is like, I hope you know what you're doing. Because it's not just about you."

Before he could respond, Jeff rode off to lead the group and Bo stared after him. His friend's words replayed in his mind and he looked down at Ella's blond head. As much as he hated to admit it, Jeff had a point. It wasn't just about him anymore. Whatever decisions he made would directly affect Ella. That was huge. If things didn't work out with Morgan, it wasn't just him that would be affected.

"Dammit."

Ella turned around, her eyes wide at Bo's curse, but she didn't say anything.

"Sorry," Bo muttered.

Bo managed an apologetic smile that Ella seemed to accept. She turned around and resumed stroking Horace's mane, murmuring words in his ear. Bo scrubbed a hand over his face and exhaled a long breath. Only a few hours ago, everything had made perfect sense and he'd allowed himself to think about the possibility of a future with both Ella and Morgan. But Jeff was right; he knew Bo better than anyone and he knew that Bo didn't do relationships. There was a reason for that. He didn't know how.

The situation was all too damn complicated. Bo inhaled deeply, desperate to fill his lungs with air. He focused on the trail in front of him and carefully avoided looking behind him, even when Morgan's sweet laughter rang through the air.

Once they returned to the Lodge, the group split up. Bo managed to hang out in the barn just long enough to avoid Morgan, who he knew had to hurry and get ready for her shift. It was a chicken move, but he didn't know what to say to her. He'd spent the rest of the ride back going over his options and the only conclusion he'd reached was that he had no clue what to do.

By the time Bo finished with his duties, Ella was asleep in a pile of blankets in the tack room. He scooped her light weight into his arms and started back to the main building. She instinctively snuggled close to him and his heart clenched. He took his time walking the trail, enjoying his daughter in his arms because only in sleep did she seem to trust him. No matter what Morgan said, Bo wasn't sure Ella had bonded with him yet. Or if she ever would.

Instead of heading straight back to the condo, Bo had to stop in the main building to sign off on the trip and check his schedule. Carmen was the first person he saw when he walked through the doors. She was talking to a woman and a man; they had their backs to him but something about the woman was familiar.

Carmen saw Bo but didn't smile. She said something to the

couple, who turned around and looked at him. Bo's first instinct was to squeeze Ella a little tighter against the penetrating stare of Clara Kersey, the social worker. He looked to the man. Bo had never seen him before, but the man's familiar brown eyes told Bo exactly who he was and more important, why he was there. Clara had found Ella's uncle.

Chapter Eighteen

IT HAD ONLY BEEN one day since they'd returned from their overnight trip, and although Bo was busy, Morgan was still hoping to see him soon after they returned. She felt like a teenager caught up in the bliss of a crush and she couldn't stop thinking about him. She couldn't wait to get down to the Cub's Club for the start of the day because of course Ella was scheduled, which meant she'd get to see two of her favorite people.

"I didn't think your shift started for another hour." Sleepy eyed, Astrid appeared from her bedroom and made a beeline to the coffeepot.

Morgan took another big gulp from her own cup and smiled. "There's nothing wrong with getting a head start on the day, is there?"

Astrid shook her head, the beads in her hair clicking together, and slumped into the chair. "The energy is just way off with you morning people. Besides, you wouldn't be nearly so perky if you'd come to the party last night. That would've settled you down a bit."

When she'd returned from her private babysitting job the night before, Astrid had tried to drag her to a party in another of the staff buildings, but Morgan had been worn out after a day on horseback and then working, so she'd begged off.

"I wasn't in the party mood," she said. "But it looks like it must have been a good one."

Astrid grabbed her head. "I have to think there's some bad spiritual karma for whoever thought beer pong was a good idea."

Morgan laughed, but handed her friend a glass of water and some Tylenol. "Take this."

Astrid dutifully swallowed the pills. "I think I would hate you for looking so good this morning if I didn't love you for taking care of me." She crossed her arms on the table and rested her head.

"Aw, I love you, too. Now go back to bed," Morgan ordered. "You don't start till three, which means you have lots of time to rest. Why are you even awake?"

"I wanted to ask you something." Astrid's voice was mumbled in her arms.

Morgan glanced at her watch. She still had time so she poured some more coffee. "What's that?"

Astrid propped her head up with one arm. "Jeff was saying something last night about Bo."

Her face immediately burned with heat, and she was sure her face was probably the same shade as the bowl of apples on the table. Her brain spun with what Jeff could have said. Surely Bo wouldn't have told his friend about them. Not before they'd even figured anything out.

"Oh?" was all Morgan could manage.

Astrid took a tentative sip of her coffee before continuing. "Yeah, and I just wondered if he'd been acting weird on the trip. The whole thing seems so strange that I couldn't even believe it when Jeff told me. But Jeff was pretty pissed about it —his aura was flaming red and black. And I've never seen it so dark. Jeff is normally a blue and green kinda guy—"

133

"Wait." It took Morgan a second to catch up with Astrid was saying. "What are you talking about?"

"He's usually so bright and vibrant." Astrid rubbed her eyes and blinked hard. "But last night he was so dark. Stormy almost."

"Jeff was?" Morgan struggled to keep up with what Astrid was talking about. "Why would he be angry? It doesn't have anything to do with him."

She hadn't realized she'd spoken aloud until Astrid said, "Jeff was pissed because he thought Bo made the wrong choice."

"With me?" Morgan blurted before she could stop herself.

Her outburst seemed to shake Astrid from her sleepy stupor. She sat up and examined Morgan. "Wait," Astrid said. "What are you talking about? Did you and Bo—"

"No."

Astrid raised an eyebrow.

"We didn't," Morgan insisted. The heat in her face grew more intense but she didn't look away. "Why would Jeff be upset about…well, whatever he was upset about."

"You don't know? I thought for sure you'd be upset too. I'm actually shocked to find you so-"

"No," she whispered, cutting Astrid off. The hair on the back of Morgan's neck stood up and a tingle of what could only be fear streaked through her landing in the pit of her stomach. Slowly, she shook her head from side to side. "Tell me."

"Bo sent Ella away."

The words reverberated through Morgan's skull before she could process them. "What? With who?" They were the only two questions she could manage to get out.

Astrid took another sip of coffee before answering. Morgan had to force herself not to rip the mug out of her friend's hand and force her to tell her everything she knew. "Some lady from

Social Services was here when they got back from the trip. I guess there was a guy with her, too."

"And they took Ella?"

Morgan's chest ached for what Bo must be going through. For them to just come and take his little girl, after everything they'd been through. And Ella. She must be terrified. Morgan put her mug on the counter, and turned to leave. She had to find Bo and help him.

"They didn't take her," Astrid said. "He gave Ella to them. I guess he'd called them and asked them to come. That's why Jeff was so angry."

Time froze as Morgan turned around and looked at Astrid. "He gave Ella to them?"

Astrid nodded. "Are you okay, Morgan?"

She nodded and rubbed absently at her arms. It couldn't be true. Bo wouldn't do that.

"Morgan?" Astrid put her hand on Morgan's arm. She hadn't even noticed that Astrid had gotten up from the table. "Do you need to sit down? You don't look so good."

Morgan shook off her friend's touch. "I'm fine," she whispered. "I have to go."

Morgan went straight to Bo's condo and banged on the door. She needed to hear it directly from him. She needed to hear him tell her that he'd sent his beautiful, broken daughter away. Disbelief had given way to anger on the short walk through the wooded trails and Morgan was ready to demand answers.

"Bo!" She hit the door again. "Let me in."

Before she could bang again, the door swung open and a girl that Morgan recognized from the staff BBQ and had only met once or twice, appeared, wearing only Bo's denim shirt over bare legs. Morgan took a shaky step backward, and swallowed hard.

"Morgan, right?" The girl leaned against the door frame and crossed her arms. "I've seen you—"

"Where's Bo?"

The girl's face hardened and she stood straight. "He's not here."

She was lying. She had to be lying. Morgan forced herself to make eye contact with the girl whose name continued to elude her. "I need to talk to him."

"That makes two of us," she said. "When you find him, you can let him know that I'm not impressed."

Morgan stumbled backwards, tripping over a rock before turning and walking down the trail. She heard the door close behind her but she didn't look back. Despite the storm brewing inside her, she still had a job to do. She needed to get to the Cub's Club. People were depending on her, and there was no point wandering around, anyway. Bo would have come to her if he'd wanted to talk about whatever it was that happened. He hadn't. And the half-naked girl—Morgan refused to let herself think about what seeing her meant. Bo didn't owe her anything. Obviously, despite what she'd thought only a short time ago, they didn't have a relationship; he could do what he wanted.

But even as she tried to rationalize it in her mind, Morgan's stomach knotted and a sense of heaviness descended on her. For just a moment, she'd allowed herself to believe that it could be possible to fall for someone. She dared to think it might work with Bo, that not only could she accept his situation, but welcome it. And maybe, they could even be a—no, she wouldn't even think the word. Because now she'd never know. As quickly as it had come, the possibility was gone. She kicked at a stray pinecone on the trail and sent it skittering into the bush.

By the time Morgan walked through the doors to the Cub's Club, she was resigned that whatever she may or may not have had with Bo was nothing more than a convenient distraction for him while he sorted things out with Ella and got back to his regular life.

"Are you okay, Morgan?" Lisa asked when Morgan wandered into the office.

Morgan nodded and took the clipboard from the desk. Only four kids were signed up for the day. Ella's name had been crossed out. Her stomach flipped and the tightness in her chest grew as she stared at the clipboard.

"Morgan?"

She blinked back the unwelcome tears and thrust the clipboard back at Lisa. "The kids should be here soon," Morgan said, changing the subject. "We should get ready."

The morning went by in a haze and for Morgan, everything felt wrong. More than once, she caught herself looking to the pile of pillows where Ella liked to curl up and nap. When the kids had popsicles, she couldn't help but think of Ella and her sticky red fingers the first time they'd met. It was crazy how in only a few short weeks, one child could wrap herself around Morgan's heart so completely. And then break it with her absence.

Thankful for Lisa, Morgan wandered from one activity to another all day, only half-heartedly engaging with the kids. She needed to snap out of it and do her job, but no matter how much she told herself she was being ridiculous, Morgan couldn't stop thinking about Bo and Ella. She remembered the way Bo had rushed into the room with Ella in his arms the day she'd tripped and skinned her knee. He'd been so concerned, so caring. How could that be the same Bo who had given his daughter to Social Services? How could the same man who had grilled Morgan for ways to connect with Ella turn around and get rid of her?

"Morgan?" Lisa's voice broke her thoughts and it took her a moment to realize that Lisa was speaking to her. She lifted a hand in response and Lisa continued, "I thought we could do some paintings with the kids today. Could you go mix them up?"

Morgan nodded her response. Normally, it would be her asking Lisa to get the supplies ready. But nothing was normal and nothing made sense. She went to the supply station and started taking the powdered paints out of the cupboard. Without measuring, Morgan dumped some blue powder in the red cup and went back to her thoughts.

The more she went over what had happened, the more questions she had. The Bo she'd gotten to know, the one she was falling in love with, wouldn't do what everyone said he'd done. But then again, she reminded herself, maybe she didn't know Bo at all. Their kisses had been passionate and deep and had definitely left her craving more. And she'd been so sure that Bo felt the same way. After all, hadn't she seen that same desire reflected in his eyes, and felt it in the way he touched her? She had. She knew she had.

A flare of anger ripped through her and she jerked back, spilling the red powder she was measuring all over the floor. "Crap!" She slammed the container down on the cupboard and tried to wipe up the mess. The powder smeared into a red smudge. "Oh, come on," Morgan said to herself and the increasing mess. Tears flooded her eyes as she stopped and stared at the mess.

"Morgan?" Lisa appeared at her side.

"I don't know what to do," Morgan whispered.

"It's just paint. It's okay." Lisa took her arm and led her to the private office.

"No, it's not okay."

Lisa sat her in the chair and handed her a tissue. "You don't seem like yourself today."

That was an understatement and they both knew it.

"I miss her, too," Lisa said softly. "If you want to talk…"

Morgan shook her head.

"Okay, well, I have everything under control out there. Why don't you just stay in here for a bit until you feel better?"

Morgan nodded and laid her head on the desk, cradling it in her arms. Of course, Lisa knew what had happened. News travelled fast at the Lodge. Everyone probably also knew about how Morgan had fallen for his act. She'd been played, by Castle Mountain's biggest player. She'd known about his reputation, and let it happen anyway. Morgan's tears fell on the desk, splashing against her skin. She'd been a fool and now, nothing made sense.

Chapter Nineteen

THE SUN WAS high in the sky by the time Bo blinked his eyes open and then instantly shut them again against the blinding light. He groaned and rubbed his palms into his gritty eyes. It wasn't like him to sleep so late; then again, it wasn't like him to drink more than his share of a bottle of tequila. Straight.

Bo groaned again and rolled over to check the time. He opened his eyes again, this time looking squarely at the trunk of a tree.

"What the—"

He pushed himself up to a sitting position and instantly regretted it as a wave of nausea swept through him. When it passed, he opened his eyes again and looked around. All he could see were pine trees and shrubs but no sign of the Lodge or any other building.

"Shit."

Memories of the night before came to him in bits and pieces. He remembered propping himself up at the bar and downing shot after shot of tequila that the bartender, Luke, poured for him. He remembered swiping the bottle when Luke said he'd had enough. And he remembered taking Taryn, the cute blond who worked at the front desk, back to his room with him. He'd known she was a sure thing. She'd wanted him since the start of the season and hadn't made a secret of it. Bo didn't particularly care for her. She wasn't his type—she wasn't Morgan.

He shut his eyes, trying in vain to close his mind to everything else. The things he didn't want to remember. The memories came hard and fast, like a slide show on fast forward. Stumbling down the path to his condo. Kissing Taryn up against the door. Opening the door to an empty suite. Empty because only hours earlier he'd packed her bags and given Ella to Clara Kersey and watched her walk away.

Ella.

The memory brought a physical stab of pain to his gut. With a cry of anguish ripping through him, Bo rolled to his knees and emptied the contents of his stomach.

Once he could move without feeling like he'd be ill again, Bo stumbled along the path, using the direction of the sun to guide him back to the Lodge. It had been the ultimate in stupidity, running out into the woods alone and at night, but Bo was pretty sure he hadn't been thinking of everything that could have gone wrong when he'd taken off from the suite. He was pretty sure he hadn't been thinking at all. Even after walking for awhile, by his estimate he was still at least an hour away, which was good because it would give him time to sober up. And think.

The tequila may have numbed his feelings for a while, but the fuzz couldn't last forever and with the alcohol slowly leaving his body, Bo had enough clarity to know that he'd made a terrible choice. The hole in his heart where Ella's presence should have been ached enough that Bo struggled to get a deep breath as he remembered the day before.

When he'd walked into the lobby with Ella in his arms, he'd been taken off guard. He'd forgotten that he'd been the one to call Clara Kersey. That he'd been the one to tell Social Services that maybe Ella's uncle would be a better guardian. A man he didn't even know. A man he'd never even spoken to. And yet, when Clara introduced them, and reminded Bo why she was there, he still didn't open his mouth to tell her that he'd changed his mind. He didn't tell her that he'd fallen in love with Ella and that he couldn't imagine not having her with him.

He didn't say any of that. Instead, Bo had let his insecurities take over. He remembered what Jeff had said about not screwing things up with Morgan. About telling him how much an unstable childhood could harm a child. So instead of following his heart, he'd looked at Ella, still asleep in his arms and was suddenly and totally overwhelmed by the responsibility of making the wrong choices with her life. In the end, he'd been a coward. He'd bent his head and placed a gentle kiss on Ella's forehead and then handed her to the uncle. The man he didn't know.

When Ella's eyes fluttered open and she'd looked at him with confusion and fear in her eyes, he'd lied to her and told her that everything would be okay. Then he'd turned away and gone to pack her bags.

He'd abandoned her. His own daughter.

With remembrance crashing through him, Bo started running. He moved his feet down the trail as fast as his exhausted body would carry him. Stumbling, tripping, and cursing, he made his laborious way through the forest, until out of breath, exhausted and tired, he arrived back at the Lodge.

Chapter Twenty

ASTRID WAS STILL at work when Morgan pushed through the door of their apartment. The last thing she needed was to explain to her roommate why she'd skipped out from her shift early. All she wanted to do was curl up in her bed and forget all about Bo and Ella and how they'd both managed to work their way into her carefully-guarded heart.

She stripped off her jeans and tossed them on the floor. A flash of red caught her eye and she bent to retrieve the sunstone that she'd tucked into her pocket earlier.

"Yeah, right," she scoffed. "Protection and attraction? So much for your stupid stone, Astrid." She started to toss the rock into the wastebasket, but stopped herself and put it on the dresser. She'd give it back to Astrid later.

She was just pulling the cover over her head when there was a banging at the door. Morgan ignored it thinking it was probably just someone who wanted to party. The problem with staff residence, she'd discovered, was that someone always wanted to party. She tugged the blanket tightly over her head and willed the knocking to stop.

"Morgan!"

Her breath caught in her throat at the sound of the voice, but she didn't move. There was nothing he could say that could explain what he'd done. Why he'd used her and then tossed his daughter aside. She willed her heart to slow its frenzied pace. She held her breath and listened.

"Open the door," Bo called. And then softer, "Please."

The catch in his voice and the pain behind the last word made Morgan throw the covers back, pull on her jeans, and go to him.

When she opened the door, Morgan's hand instinctively reached out to Bo. His handsome face was covered in dirt and it looked like tear tracks had streaked through the grime on his cheeks. His eyes were bloodshot; his clothes were ripped and covered with grass and leaves.

"Are you okay?" she asked. Her hands flew over him, not touching, but assessing the damage.

"I let her go," he said, ignoring her question.

Morgan stepped back as he walked forward into her apartment and she had to hold a hand to her face to protect against the stench of alcohol wafting off him.

"Bo...you...what the hell happened?" She finally settled on a question.

He didn't answer right away. Instead, he walked through the room and sank on to the couch. Morgan crossed her arms and leaned up against the wall. A wave of rage so sudden and so intense filled her, scaring her with its intensity. She wanted to tell him to leave. Tell him to get his alcohol-soaked, cheating, child-abandoning self out of her apartment. He'd hurt her. She'd trusted him with her heart and he'd thrown it away. She wanted to yell and scream at him. But watching him sitting on her couch, broken and defeated by his own demons, she also wanted to help him and the rage melted as quickly as it'd appeared.

Morgan filled a glass of water and put it in his hand. She

held all her questions and waited while he drank deep. When he was ready, he handed her the empty glass and cleared his throat.

"I gave her away," he said. She swallowed hard against the painful tightening in her throat, but didn't say anything. "I got scared, Morgan." He looked up at her, his eyes shadowed and weary. "I was selfish and scared and I let them take her." His voice hitched and a tear slipped from his eye. "I have to get her back. I need to get her back. I didn't realize until it was too late what I'd done. But Morgan, I fell in love."

Morgan's heart skipped a beat at his words even though he wasn't talking about her. She swallowed all the things she wanted to say to him but couldn't. Instead, she forced herself to smile. "Of course you did," she said. "You fell in love with a sweet little blond girl. You fell in love with your daughter."

Morgan prepared a pot of tea while Bo made the call to Clara Kersey. She listened from the kitchen while he explained to the Social Services lady how he'd panicked at the thought of being a father, and apologized for wasting everyone's time. Morgan could feel her own heart break a little more as Bo fought back tears while he spoke, but when he finally hung up, he had a cautious smile on his face.

"She agreed to meet," he said. Morgan put a cup of tea on the table in front of him. "Tessa's brother has a family of his own and his wife wasn't thrilled about the daughter of his estranged sister coming to live with them, so Clara still feels that I'm the best person to raise Ella." A sheepish grin spread across his face. "Even if I did screw up a little bit."

"You did," Morgan said. "But no parent is perfect."

He shook his head. "No, I guess not. And I still have a lot to learn." He ran his hands through his hair, leaving it standing at wild angles. "And it's still not a sure thing," he said. "Clara said that there'll be paperwork and lots of questions. Of course, they'll need to be sure that it's a permanent solution this time."

Morgan raised an eyebrow. "And is it?"

He dropped his hands and leapt to his feet. "Of course!"

"I'm sorry," Morgan looked down, "I wasn't trying to…"

"No," Bo said. He dropped to a crouch in front of her and took her hand. A spark flew through her, but Morgan worked to control her response before he saw it. "I'm sorry," he said. "I know you're just trying to help, and I suppose it was a fair question."

Morgan nodded, careful not to move her hand. She enjoyed the feel of his skin on hers. It was difficult to believe that only twenty-four hours ago that same action had felt normal and easy between them. Too soon, Bo released her hand and sat again. She tried not to let the disappointment show on her face. The last thing Bo was going to worry about was a relationship with her. He needed to focus on getting his little girl back, and so did she.

Morgan forced herself to take a sip of tea and slow her racing heart before asking, "Did she say how Ella's doing?"

Bo's face fell. "Clara said Ella won't speak at all and she's slept a lot."

Morgan nodded. "That doesn't surprise me," she said. "But she'll be okay. Once she's back with you."

"And you."

She froze, the teacup halfway to her lips. Hope and uncertainty fluttered through her. "Me?"

Bo opened his mouth to say something, but stopped himself. He took a drink of his tea and then said, "At the Cub's Club. She'll be with you there, and Ella just loves you so much, it'll be good for her."

Morgan looked down, desperate for the disappointment

she felt to not show on her face. This wasn't about her or whatever it was she thought she had been developing with Bo. Morgan swallowed hard. She needed to put her feelings aside for Ella's sake.

Unable to sit across from him any longer, Morgan pushed up from the couch and collected the empty teacups. "More tea?" she asked.

"No," he said, "I should probably go get cleaned up and get moving if I'm going to get to the city in time."

Without turning around, Morgan nodded. She needed him to leave. To get out of her space so she could breathe again. Every time she looked at him, her heart hurt a little more and her stomach clenched tighter against the pain of being tossed aside. Only hours ago, it had been easier to be angry with him. But now that she'd seen him and seen his own anguish at what he'd done, the anger was gone, replaced with heartache.

She still had so many unanswered questions for Bo. But she couldn't ask any of them yet. Maybe never. And it no longer mattered. Clearly, Bo didn't feel the same way. That was evident by the half-naked girl in his condo. Morgan took a deep breath and fortified herself. No, she wouldn't say anything. Bo needed to focus on Ella. On being a parent. A problem she knew all too well that she would never have.

"Morgan?"

She froze at the soft touch of his hand on her shoulder. She didn't want to turn around. Didn't want him to see the hurt that undoubtedly shone in her eyes. "Yes?"

He moved her slowly, so he was looking straight in her eyes. One look at him, and Morgan could see that all of his energy was focused on Ella. Whatever she was feeling about their relationship was most definitely one-sided. She blinked hard, waiting for him to speak.

"Will you come with me?" He spoke the question so softly, and with so much need that she couldn't say no.

Chapter Twenty-One

BO DIDN'T KNOW how Morgan would react when he'd asked her to come with him, but he did know he couldn't imagine making the trip without her. Without even thinking about it, or wanting it, Morgan had slipped into his life.

He snuck a glance at the passenger seat and looked at Morgan, really looked at her, for the first time since the craziness had started. She looked tired, as if she hadn't slept, and there was something different about her. A sadness. Bo felt a flash of guilt and turned away. He wasn't stupid. He'd done that to her. He'd made her sad.

After having time to think about it, he'd decided that it hadn't been fair for him to kiss her at the campfire and then continue their, whatever it was, at Forgotten Falls. He was smart enough to know that she was as attracted to him as he was to her, and it wasn't right for him to act on it when he couldn't follow through. And he couldn't follow through. Not when he didn't know how.

"So what do you think will happen now?" Morgan asked, pulling him out of his thoughts. It took him a few minutes to realize that she was talking about Ella and not the two of them.

"I don't know," he said. "Obviously I hope that I'll be able to have full custody. But I know that it won't be as easy as it was before. I really screwed up when I let her go."

At the memory of Ella's scared eyes when he'd walked away, Bo's stomach turned and he pressed down on the gas pedal a little harder.

"Why did you do it?" Morgan asked the question he'd been hoping to avoid. The atmosphere in the car charged up and she asked again. "Why would you let her go?"

He swallowed hard. She deserved an answer. After all, he'd involved her in this whether she'd wanted to be or not. "I got scared," he said.

"Scared?" Bo could feel her eyes on him, and he had to force himself to keep his eyes on the road. He didn't think he could face her when he told her the truth. "That's what you said earlier, but I still can't believe that you gave your child to a stranger because you got scared."

"I don't blame you if you think I'm a coward," he started.

"A coward? I don't think you're a coward at all," she said, her voice much softer. Bo risked another look at her. Morgan's eyes glistened with tears and he felt another pang in his chest at the thought that he had put them there.

"Morgan, I—"

"Bo. You didn't even know you had a daughter and hours later you were a father. To a four-year-old girl. That couldn't have been easy, but you did it. A coward would have turned her away from the very beginning." Morgan was twisted around in her seat, speaking with so much passion that for a minute, Bo believed her. "You did what you could, and you did good."

"It doesn't change the fact that I gave her away." Emotion choked him. He was thankful that he was driving and had something else to focus on. He didn't want to cry in front of Morgan. Not again.

"You did," she said. "And I still don't understand why. But it happened and you can't change it now. But, Bo—"

He looked at her, taking his eyes off the road just long enough to see the unguarded expression on her face. "You are not a coward," she continued. "Think of everything you've been through and everything you're doing right now."

He didn't want to look away; he wanted to see her looking at him like that forever. But when he turned back to the road and then glanced at Morgan again, her face was once more carefully masked leaving him to think that maybe he'd imagined it.

Bo had never felt more like a reprimanded child than he did at that moment, sitting in booth across from Clara Kersey. In fact, even as a child, Bo was pretty sure he'd never felt quite so chastised. Sitting in front of her as she explained to him the responsibilities of being a parent, Bo had to bite his lip and take the tongue-lashing like a man, because he knew in his heart that he deserved every minute of it.

He looked to the empty seat next to him in the roadside diner and wished that Morgan had come in with him. He would have liked her support, her hand on his next to him, her warm smile making him feel more at ease. Really, he would have just enjoyed her presence close to him. But when he'd asked her to come in, she declined with a shake of her head and said she'd wait outside. "Ella is your family, Bo," she'd said. "Not mine."

Those last two words had squished Bo's heart, but he didn't have time to ask her what she meant. Heck, he knew exactly what she meant.

"Mr. Clancy," Clara was still speaking, dragging him back to the present. "A child as vulnerable as Ella cannot withstand much more of this being jostled around. You will have to make a decision, one that we will agree to, of course," she added, almost as an afterthought.

"Of course," Bo agreed. "Ms. Kersey, please believe me when I tell you that I have no intention of ever letting Ella out of my sight again. In fact, I fully intend to be the best father I can be." He looked again to Ella, sitting in the corner of the booth, picking at a plate of French fries. "I'm Ella's dad," he said, liking the way it sounded, "and I have full intentions for us to be a family forever. I plan to do everything in my power to make sure she's happy and healthy from now on."

He turned back to the social worker, whose mouth was set in a thin line. "You do sound convincing."

"That's because I mean every word," Bo said as emphatically as he could without sounding as though he was a total lunatic.

"As I told you before, Mr. Clancy, it's always our first goal to place children with immediate family. We do believe that blood relatives are the best place for children. It seems that Ella's uncle, while willing to step up and take responsibility, has his own family issues. As you can see, I've asked him not to be here, and because it was her mother's wish for her to be with you, he does agree that it would probably be the best place for Ella. But," she held her hand up when Bo moved to speak, "it is also a priority for the children to be placed in stable homes. Preferably homes where there is both a mother and a father."

Bo's mind flashed to Morgan, but quickly pushed the thought from his mind.

"But failing that," Clara continued, "we really just want what's best for the child." She glanced down at Ella, who had stuck a fry in her mouth and was watching Bo warily, as if he'd take off again. "And I think we both know that a placement with her biological father would be best."

Bo nodded, but caught himself. He didn't want to seem too

eager. Even if he did want to shout from the rooftops that he was a daddy.

"There will be spot checks, Mr. Clancy." Clara was still talking. Bo wanted to grab Ella and go. He wanted to get on with his life. This time, properly. But that couldn't happen until Clara Kersey said the word. He smiled and nodded.

Something over his head caught Clara's attention, and then Ella's. The little girl immediately sat up, her plate of fries forgotten. "Morgan."

It was the first thing Ella had said since Bo had sat down. It must have been the first thing she'd said in a while because even Clara looked shocked.

Bo turned around and his eyes took her in. She'd been crying. Bo could see that right away and a pang went through him. His selfishness had caused too much pain for everyone. And it physically hurt him to think of how he'd affected those he cared about. He tried to catch her eye, but Morgan was trying very hard to avoid looking at them. She peered around the small diner and then started walking through the tables, toward the bathrooms at the back of the room.

"Morgan," Ella said again, this time louder, and Morgan heard her. She froze and turned slowly. Bo watched as her face transformed into a warm smile, directed straight at Ella.

"A friend of yours?" Clara asked.

Bo nodded. "Morgan," he called out to her. "Please, come meet Clara Kersey."

For a moment, she hesitated and Bo was afraid she'd decline. But then her eyes locked on Ella's and a smile crossed her face. In the next moment, she crossed the floor and came to stand in front of the booth.

Bo stood and made the introductions. "Would you like a coffee?" he asked Morgan.

Her face flushed and she shook her head. "Oh no," Morgan said. "I really don't want to interrupt. I know this is family business and I…" She glanced toward the bathroom. "I really just had to come in to use the facilities. It was nice to meet you, Ms. Kersey." Morgan looked back to Ella and took her hand across the table. "And I hope I'll be seeing you really soon, kiddo."

Both Ella and Morgan's face lit up with happiness at the contact and Bo felt a surge of…what? Happiness? Excitement? He couldn't pinpoint the feeling, but as Morgan left them, heading towards the back of the diner, he did know that he needed that woman to stop walking away, because more than ever, he wanted her to stay.

Chapter Twenty-Two

IT HAD BEEN A LONG DAY, and when Bo finally pulled the car into the staff parking lot at the Lodge, Morgan was relieved it was over. She'd dozed a little on the way back from the city, but it was difficult to let herself relax enough to sleep when there was so much tension between her and Bo.

"You'll be okay?" Morgan asked, referring to Ella who was asleep in the back seat, her clay deer clutched in her hand. Bo had brought it to her at the diner, and Ella hadn't let it go since. Morgan turned and watched Ella, lost in the gentle rise and fall of her chest and the simple beauty of a child sleeping.

She startled when Bo touched her arm. "I'll be fine," he said softly in her ear. "I have everything I need."

A shiver ran through her. From his touch or his words, she couldn't be sure. The last few hours with him had been a sweet torture for Morgan. She'd wanted to be with him, close to him, talking, touching, just being. But at the same time she knew it would never be.

She placed her hand atop his and turned to face him. His handsome features were blurred by exhaustion. But he looked happy, too. The type of happiness that goes straight to the soul.

He had his little girl back, and that was all he needed. All that mattered.

Morgan managed a small smile and squeezed his hand. "You will be okay," she said and before he could say anything else, Morgan added, "As long as you love her hard, you'll be okay."

"Love hard?"

"My mom always used to say that if you loved hard enough, all the other stuff wouldn't matter. Or at least, it would matter less." Morgan pulled her hand away and held it in her lap. "And I think for you, right now, you need to love really hard and all the other stuff that's happened won't matter anymore."

"Love hard," Bo repeated the words to himself. "I like it." The smile on his face lit him up and for the first time since she'd met him, Morgan thought he looked content.

"I'm going to go." She slipped her hand to the door handle and made her escape. He didn't try to stop her, but she didn't think he would. He was completely lost in his daughter.

Morgan managed to sidestep a party that was going on in the first floor of the resident apartments and slip up to the second story. She was just about to put the key in her lock when a voice stopped her.

"Did you talk some sense into him?"

Morgan turned to see Jeff, his bulk propped against the wall at the end of the corridor. He had a beer in his hand, and by the sway in his posture and the droop of his eyelids, it wasn't his first.

She tucked the key in her pocket. "What?"

He pushed off the wall and made his way toward her. When he came to stand next to her, he slumped against the wall and took a deep pull of his beer. "Did you talk some sense into that fool friend of mine?"

Morgan turned and crossed her arms against her chest. "You mean—"

"Ella." Jeff took another swig of beer and nodded. "Stupidest thing he ever did. Children shouldn't be given away so easily. Just handed back and forth like they're nothing more than—"

He stopped and his features clouded over but Morgan couldn't be sure whether it was the beer or something deeper going on.

"He freaked," Jeff said after a moment. "I guess I can't blame him, but…it sucks. She was a cute kid and so good for him. Just what he needed. I've never seen him so settled than when we were up at the cabin and he was with the two of you. It would have been good. But now—"

"Wait," Morgan said, taking a minute to catch up. "You haven't spoken to him?"

"Not since right after that woman came to take Ella." Jeff tipped his head and finished his beer. "And that coward let her go." He crunched the can easily in his fist.

Morgan reached out and put her hand over his until the tension released. "He got her back, Jeff," she said. "He went and got her back."

It took a moment before her words sank into Jeff's alcohol-clouded brain, but when they did, he looked at her and burst into tears. He opened his hand and pulled her close to him into a tight embrace. He was strong and smelled distinctly like a brewery, but she let him have his cry.

When his tears subsided, Morgan eased out of his grip. "I didn't think it mattered so much to you," she said with a smile.

"Ah, ignore me." Jeff swiped at his face. "I'm a bit of a softie for this type of thing and, well…"

"You've been drinking," Morgan finished for him. "That

does seem to be the way to handle problems with you boys," she muttered under her breath, and then added, "Come on. Let's get you a coffee."

Morgan had already accepted that she wouldn't be having the quiet evening alone, drowning her troubles in too much ice cream, that she wanted. So when she opened the door and saw Astrid lounging on the couch, it didn't much matter that her roommate wasn't out at the party either.

"You're home," Astrid said as she twisted around. "And you look like shit. What's wrong?" She hopped off the sofa and came to meet Morgan at the door. "Your energy is way off," Astrid said. Her hands flew over Morgan, hovering only inches away from her skin. "What happened?"

"What the?" Jeff pushed through the space between them and forced Astrid to take a few steps back. "Of course she looks like shit. Sorry, Morgan," he said to her before turning back to Astrid. "Bo has been completely screwing things up again."

"With Ella? I knew that, but...oh," Astrid looked back and forth from one face to the other. "Bo?"

Morgan nodded slightly.

"I knew it," Astrid said with a touch of triumph. "You said it was nothing, but you were putting out love vibes big time."

"I don't—"

"Come, tell me everything." Astrid grabbed Morgan's arm and dragged her to the table.

"Well, he didn't sleep with Taryn," Astrid said and sat back in her chair.

Morgan had been filling her roommate in on all the details of the last few weeks, including her growing feelings for Bo. To be fair, Astrid had mostly figured those out on her own. She had some sort of sixth sense for that type of thing anyway, so there was no point in trying to deny it. By the time Morgan had gotten to the part of the story where she'd met the half-naked girl at Bo's condo, she was so tired, she almost didn't hear what Astrid had said.

"What?" It was Jeff who asked, his mouth hanging open in disbelief. "He took Taryn home?" He shook his head.

"Why do you seem so shocked?" Astrid asked. "She's a total cutie."

Jeff sat back and folded his arms over his chest. Sometime over the past hour, he'd sobered up enough to be part of the conversation. "Yeah, Taryn's a hottie for sure. But I'm confused about his taking anyone home at all."

"Really?" Astrid cocked her head and laughed. "Because the Bo I know—"

"He's changed," Jeff interrupted. "I've known Bo a long time and I've never seen him as settled as I have in the last few weeks. It's different, I'm telling you."

"Wait," Morgan jumped in. Her head was spinning from exhaustion and everything she'd heard. She focused on Astrid. "What did you mean, he didn't sleep with her?"

"Taryn? I don't know what happened, but she was busy bitching about it to anyone who'd listen," Astrid said. "It's no secret that she's been trying to get him for the last few years, but he's had no time for her. Apparently, he's the one who suggested they go back to his place, but…"

"What?" Morgan needed to hear it.

"When they got there, he freaked out and ran off."

"Freaked out?"

"I knew he wouldn't sleep with her," Jeff said. "He was drunk and totally out of his head."

"There's a lot of that going around, I see," Astrid said, giving him a pointed look.

Confusion and unanswered questions swirled through

Morgan's head and she rested it in her hands on the table. "I don't know what to think anymore. I just don't know what to do."

"I think that's obvious," Astrid said.

Morgan looked up to see her friends exchanging knowing looks. "What?" she demanded. "What's so obvious?"

"You need to talk to him."

"I can't." Morgan shook her head. "No, he has too much to worry about right now. Ella needs to come first."

"And she will," Jeff said. He put his hand on her shoulder and squeezed. "But I know him. Bo needs you, too."

"I don't—"

"Go," Astrid said. "You need to talk to him. Tell him how you feel."

Morgan shook her head. "I want to, but…"

Astrid's eyes locked on hers. "Whatever it is holding you back," she said, "let it go. Or you'll regret it forever."

Chapter Twenty-Three

FOR A MOMENT, Bo considered waking Ella up when he carried her from the back seat of the car and put her in the bed. He wanted to talk to her. He wanted to tell her how sorry he was for letting her go with Clara Kersey. He wanted to hug her and have her hug him back. Or at the least, feel her little hand clasped around his fingers.

He settled for watching her sleep after he tucked her into the big hotel room bed. He sat on the end of the mattress and watched her eyelids flutter and her chest rise and fall with each deep breath. She was home now, and that's all that mattered.

Except it wasn't home. The unwelcome thought hit him as he looked around the room. A little girl's room should be full of color. Pinks, purples, yellows and greens. Not beige. Pictures of rainbows, horses, bunnies—or whatever it was that little girls liked—should be everywhere. Not professionally-done, mass-produced landscapes adorning the walls. Bo shook his head. A hotel room was no place for a child. It was a temporary solution, but the time for temporary was over.

A knock on the door caught his attention and he slipped out of Ella's room, pulling the door shut behind him. He could think of only one person who would be coming to see him, and his heart raced faster at the thought of seeing Morgan again. Even though he'd just left her, it had been too long. Besides, he had a lot he needed to say to her, too. No one should have to be so patient, and put up with so much from one man. He'd been self absorbed and a jerk, and he had a lot of explaining to do. He just hoped it wasn't too late.

He swung the door to the condo open, his smile melting off his face when he saw it wasn't Morgan at all.

"Hello, Bo," Carmen said. "I brought you some dinner." She held up the tray she was holding as if he hadn't been able to see it.

"Um, thanks." He stepped to the side to make room for her to enter. "I don't want to sound rude, but, why are you here?"

Carmen walked through the condo and placed the tray on the kitchen island before she turned to face him. "I want to help."

Bo didn't say anything. There had to be a catch.

"There's no catch," she said, reading his mind. "I really do want to help. I heard about Ella and I really am glad you got her back."

Bo searched her face for any indication that she was trying to trick him. "Thank you," he said cautiously. "I'm glad, too."

"Have you thought about what you're going to do now?"

That was it. Carmen had come to kick him out of the suite. Of course, it couldn't last forever and it was his own damn fault that he hadn't thought of a plan. He refused to look away from her. He forced his face into a hard line. If she were going to force him and his daughter out onto the street, he sure as hell wasn't going to go quietly.

"Don't look so angry," she said. "I'm not kicking you out. I told you—I want to help."

It took him a minute to let her words sink in. "You're not kicking me out?"

"No." She shook her head. "But you do know that you can't stay here forever. I will have to rent it out soon."

He nodded and then with the final bit of bravado draining from him, Bo sank to the couch. "I don't know where to go," he admitted. He watched as Carmen's face split into a smile.

"But I do," she said.

By the time he walked Carmen to the door half an hour later, Bo's head was spinning as he tried to absorb everything she'd told him.

"Think about it," she said, not for the first time. "The cabin's just sitting there."

Bo reached around her for the door handle. "And management agreed to let me stay there?"

"Rent it," Carmen clarified. "And of course provide the labor to fix it up." Carmen moved to leave. "Look," she said, "I know it's a lot to take in right now when you have so much going on. But it's a real option. At least for now."

It *was* an option. Bo hadn't even considered the small caretaker cabin. No one ever gave it any thought. Built almost one hundred years ago, it was a two-bedroom log house that the family that used to maintain the grounds for the Lodge had lived in. Over the years, it had seen occasional upkeep, but mostly it had fallen into disrepair.

"Thank you, Carmen," he said. "I mean it. You didn't have to do this."

She shrugged and gave him a small smile. "No, I didn't. But I see how you are with her. And I think you're both so good for each other. What you both need is a family."

"She's an amazing girl." While he spoke, Bo stared out into the darkness beyond his door. "Ella has totally changed my life."

"She has," Carmen said, "but who said I was talking about Ella?"

Bo snapped his head around so he could look her in the eyes but Carmen didn't offer an explanation; she simply shrugged again and laughed. "Good night, Bo."

Long after she'd left, Bo stood with the door open, letting the fresh mountain air soothe him. Morgan. She'd totally filled his thoughts. At least when he wasn't thinking about Ella and how to be a good dad. But there was so much more to think about. Hell, there was a lot more to think about and Bo couldn't remember there ever being a time when he'd been more excited to experience more. A lot more. A life with Ella in it would be more. So much more. And so would a life with Morgan. No matter what Jeff said, what anyone said, Bo wouldn't screw it up because it was everything he never knew he wanted. And he wanted Morgan. If it wasn't too late.

He sighed, and took another look down the dimly lit pathway that led to the Lodge and farther, to the staff quarters where Morgan was. The pull to go to her was strong. Maybe if he could just explain everything, she'd understand and give him another chance? But that wasn't an option, not with his little girl asleep inside.

Bo turned and closed the door behind him. He'd have to wait until morning before he could see her. Until then he was pretty sure he would spend a restless night thinking of all the things he was going to say to her, the things she'd say back and all the ways he'd like to make up when they were done talking.

Those thoughts finally helped Bo drift off to sleep. He dreamed of Morgan holding him close, the taste of her on his lips, and the sound of his name on her lips.

He lurched awake in bed and scanned the room.

Morgan.

Chapter Twenty-Four

BEFORE SHE COULD THINK TWICE about what she was about to do, or even think it through again, Morgan jogged down the path towards Bo's condo and straight up to the door. Astrid and Jeff had convinced her to go after what she wanted, and even with all his idiosyncrasies and his issues that he still had to deal with, Bo was undoubtedly what she wanted. She could sit back and let this great man and his beautiful daughter pass her by, or she could go and fight for what she wanted. And she intended to fight.

Morgan barely took a breath before she banged her fist on the front door. She couldn't give herself time to chicken out or rethink what she was doing. When he didn't answer, she raised her fist again and banged three times, hard. "Bo!"

Part of her told her to walk away, to make him come to her. But Morgan had had enough of playing it safe, of waiting for things to happen. It was time to make things happen.

"Bo!" She knocked her fist against the door again but before she could call for him a third time the door swung open.

Morgan had been so fired up about storming over to Bo's condo and confronting him that she hadn't given much thought to what she'd actually say when he answered the door. Especially if he answered the door wearing nothing but pajama bottoms, with his hair tousled from sleep and looking hotter than hell.

"Morgan." He half whispered, half spoke her name as if he wasn't sure it was her standing on his doorstep in the middle of the night or an apparition. "What are you...why are you..."

His confusion was enough for Morgan to regain her senses and put thoughts of running her hands down Bo's naked chest out of her mind. She shook her head and remembered why she'd come. "I need answers, Bo." She pushed past him with a gentle shove and walked into the living room. She didn't have to look to know that he'd follow.

"Morgan, I—"

"No." She held up her hand to ward off his protests. She hoped he didn't notice the way it shook, just a little, from her nerves. "I have something to say, and I need to say it." She took a deep breath. "I wasn't even going to come here tonight. I know you have a lot going on with Ella and probably the last thing on your mind right now is having a relationship with me. Hell, from what I understand, having a relationship is never the first thing on your mind."

"Morgan, that's—"

"Let me finish." She shook her head and wouldn't look in his eyes. "I know the rumors, Bo. Everyone knows that you're a player. Didn't you tell me yourself that you don't 'do relationships'?. I get it. I do." She turned away and paced the length of the room. "And you know what? I didn't want a relationship, either," she said into the picture window. "I came here to get away from all that. But then you were...well, you were..."

"What?" Bo had moved across the room so he stood right behind her. He was so close that she could feel his breath on her neck. Her entire body tightened in response to his proximity. "I was all what, Morgan?"

She held her breath but didn't dare turn around.

"Say it," he challenged her.

"You were perfect," she said. And then she did turn around. "You were so damned perfect."

Bo frowned and looked away. "I'm far from perfect, Morgan. I've done nothing but screw everything up my whole life. Look at Ella. Look at what happened there. You can't call that perfect."

"You're perfect for me," she said. "Everything that makes you who you are makes you perfect for who I am. I didn't want to fall in love with you." Morgan laughed. "I didn't even want to like you. That first day I met you, I didn't think I'd ever met someone so pompous and full of themselves as you. But then seeing you with Ella...the way you tried so hard...the way you changed everything for her. Your total willingness to change everything for one little girl, I—"

"Wait." Bo looked up and straight into her eyes, holding her gaze. "What did you say?"

"Ella—"

"Not Ella," he said. "What you said about me. Loving me."

Morgan swallowed hard. She hadn't meant to lay her feelings out so openly. She'd been caught up in the moment and until the second the words came out of her mouth, she didn't even realize herself that she felt that way. But she did. And because she'd already said it, she might as well own it.

She looked him square in the eyes and with only a slight waver in her voice said, "I just told you I've fallen in love with you. I didn't mean to, and Lord knows I can think of a thousand reasons why I shouldn't have, but I did and—"

Morgan's words were lost when Bo leaned forward and sealed his mouth to hers. Before she could think to push him away so she could finish what she needed to say, Morgan lost herself in the kiss. It no longer mattered that she had a list of things she wanted to say to him, explanations she wanted him to give her. Nothing mattered, except the taste of his lips on hers, the heat from his chest as he pressed it closer to her, and the way her body responded to him.

Bo pulled away, breaking their heat. Morgan let out a moan of displeasure and stepped back.

"Morgan," he started, "before this goes any further, I need to tell you something."

"I know you didn't sleep with Taryn."

His face twisted into a mask of confusion. "Taryn? Of course I didn't sleep with her. Did you...oh, you did."

She waved her hand, dismissing it. "Only for a minute. Astrid and Jeff sorted it out. But I still don't understand why you turned to her and why you did what you did."

"With Ella?" Bo reached for her hand and led her to the couch. "That's what I need to talk to you about. You deserve an explanation. And something tells me that as much as you like kissing me, that's the real reason you came here tonight." He smiled and it was so sexy and playful all at once that Morgan didn't have a chance to feel embarrassed.

"You're right," she said. "And I don't think I'm the only one who was enjoying the kissing." She shot him a look and crossed her arms across her chest. "So, talk."

"I see you're not going to make this easy on me."

"Should I?"

Bo shook his head slightly and looked down at his hands. "I got scared," he said after a moment. "I know I keep saying that but it's the truth. And really, there's not a whole lot more I can say. This is all so new to me, Morgan, and just like you, I didn't plan to fall in love with you. But I did."

Morgan took in a sharp breath of air and held it. She couldn't be sure that she'd heard him right. Had he really just told her he loved her? When he looked up, and she saw the emotion shining in his eyes, the truth was in front of her. She had heard him right, and he had meant it. She exhaled the breath she'd been holding.

"But it's not so simple anymore," Bo continued. "It's not just me that I need to think of and when I started to have those feelings, I panicked. What if you didn't feel the same? What if you did and it worked for a while and then I screwed it up? What about Ella? She doesn't deserve to go through that."

"So you sent her away? How is that better? How is that what's best for her? You're her father." Morgan jumped up from the couch and paced to the window again. She stared out into the darkness, searching for something. "Do you have any idea what I would give to have a child?" She whispered the question more to her reflection in the glass than to Bo. She watched his reflection as he came to stand behind her, close but not touching. "All I've ever wanted was to be a mom." Morgan spoke but didn't turn around. "I wanted to hold a child in my arms, to be her everything and know that she was mine. When I came here, I thought I could never have that, that I'd never know that love." Morgan turned. Tears streamed down her face as she continued, "And then I met Ella. I think I fell in love with her just as much as I fell in love with you. And then you...you—"

"I screwed up," Bo whispered. With a gentle touch, he used his thumb to wipe a tear off her cheek. "I can't tell you how sorry I am, Morgan. And I'm going to spend the rest of my life making it up to Ella. I got scared and I know that's not an excuse. But it's the only explanation I have."

Her chest ached with emotion for this man and his child. Morgan tipped her head and looked into Bo's eyes. "You did screw up," she said with a small smile.

"Morgan, I'm so sorry, I really am. How can I make it up to you?"

A spark lit deep in her core at his suggestion. She could

think of more than a few ways he could make amends and she was about to tell him so, when a small voice interrupted them.

"Dad?"

Both Bo and Morgan turned towards Ella, who was standing in the hallway, her hair mussed from sleep, her clay deer clutched in her hand.

"Did she just…"

Morgan's face split into a smile as she looked to Bo's shocked expression. "I think she did," she said.

"Dad," Ella said again; this time her voice was a little stronger, a bit clearer.

"Did we wake you?" Bo walked towards her and crouched so he could look into her eyes. "I'm sorry if we were too loud. I was just telling Morgan how happy I was that you're back home with me." Bo smiled and turned so he was facing Morgan, too. "Of course," he said, "I'm happy you're both here with me. And I was just going to tell Morgan a secret, but now that you're awake, I think maybe you should hear it, too." Bo turned back to Ella. "Do you want to hear my secret?"

Ella nodded frantically and Bo laughed before taking her hand and settling on the couch with her in his lap. Morgan joined them, sitting slightly apart before Bo bridged the gap between them with his hand and pulled her closer.

"So what's the secret?" Morgan asked.

"Well, we can't stay in the condo forever," Bo said. "Carmen's going to kick us out soon."

Morgan opened her mouth to protest, to tell him that he could move into staff quarters and share an apartment with her, but he held up his hand and the grin on his face stopped her from speaking.

"But I don't want to move to the city," Bo continued. "Besides, there aren't any horses in the city." Ella's eyes grew wide at the mention of horses. "So, we're going to move into our very own little cabin," Bo said triumphantly. "You'll even get your own room, Ella. Maybe we can paint it pink." Ella frowned. "Or maybe just decorate it with horses," he added quickly. "It's pretty run down right now, so we'll have to put some work into it. But it's nothing I can't handle—besides, the end result will be worth it."

"That sounds great, Bo. I'm so happy for you," Morgan said.

"Happy for us." Bo held her other hand and looked at her so intensely Morgan was afraid she might blush. "I want you to move in with us," he added. "I don't want to screw it up again, Morgan. And I won't. I promise."

The feeling drained from her hands and for a moment, Morgan felt as if she was floating. Only Bo's hands held her to the couch and to reality. Moving in together was a huge step; she wasn't sure she was ready. It was a lot to ask and even more for her to take in all at once.

Before she could give her answer, Morgan felt a tap on her shoulder. When she looked over, Ella was standing next to the couch holding the picture she'd been working on in the Cub's Club a week ago. It was the project where Morgan had the kids collect things from nature to create a scene. At the time, she hadn't given much thought to Ella's picture. She'd worked like the rest of the kids, gluing and creating. Now, with it in front of her, tears sprang to her eyes.

"Me," Ella said, pointing to the little twig girl on the paper. "Dad." She pointed to the taller figure standing next to it.

Morgan glanced over and saw the smile on Bo's face at the sound of Ella calling him Dad. Morgan was pretty sure he'd never get sick of hearing the sound of it.

"And you," Ella said, pulling Morgan's attention back to the picture. Ella's finger was pointing at the other figure standing on the other side of the little girl. She had moss for hair, but other than that, it didn't look any different from the others. When Morgan looked up, Ella was smiling one of the biggest smiles she'd seen.

"I didn't know you still had this," Morgan said as she took the picture from Ella.

"It was gonna be a gift," she said. "I hid it." Ella glanced toward her father.

"It's beautiful, Ella," Bo said.

"Hidden gifts," Morgan mused, thinking back to what Astrid had said when she'd first arrived.

"They're the best kind," Bo said.

Morgan looked first to Ella and then to Bo. "Yes," she said. "They really are." Morgan took Ella's hand and pulled her close so she could scoop her up onto her lap.

"So?" Bo asked. "What do you say? Are you ready for this?"

Balancing Ella on one knee, Morgan leaned forward and put a soft kiss on Bo's lips before pulling back. "Where do I sign up?"

I hope you loved Bo and Morgan's story (and of course little Ella's, too!) The love at the Lodge doesn't end here!
Do you remember Eva, one of Morgan's old bosses and friends? Well...she's about to meet her match with a very handsome cowboy! But only if they can get out of their own way!
Read their story in Mistaken Gifts. You can read a sneak peak of their story right after this...

And if you want even more romance...click HERE for an exclusive FREE novella that isn't available anywhere else!

Mistaken Gifts

***Please enjoy an excerpt from Mistaken Gifts, the next
in the Castle Mountain Lodge Series***

With one hand, Eva Andrews navigated the snowy mountain
road that led to Castle Mountain Lodge, while she reached for
her cell phone and hit the bluetooth button, answering the call.
If Andi was with her, she would have lectured her about
distracted driving, and yes, Eva knew she should probably
focus on the road, but she never could ignore a ringing phone.
It could be a client for their Party Hearty business, and making
clients wait wasn't good business.

But it wasn't a client's voice that came on the line.

"Hey babe," Liam's confident and slightly cocky voice,
boomed over the speaker system of the car. Eva tried not to
roll her eyes at the nickname he'd given her, but a small smile
tugged at her lips, too. They'd only been dating a little over a
month, but as independent as she was, Eva had to admit, she
liked the way he took charge of any situation, even if it was
with a lame nickname. Sometimes a girl liked to feel taken
care of.

"Hey yourself," she said, her voice laced with flirtation. "It's about time you called me back. I still need an answer about next weekend."

"Remind me again," he said. "What's next weekend?"

Eva swallowed her sigh. "My friends are getting married, remember. Andi and Collin? I thought I'd mentioned it." She probably should have been more annoyed, but it was possible in all the planning she'd been doing for the big day, she'd forgotten to mention the fact that she wanted Liam to come up to the Lodge for the weekend and be her date.

It was a big step, but she wasn't getting any younger and he'd have to meet her friends sooner or later.

"Oh yeah," he said, "you did mention it and you know I'd love to meet your friends, babe. But—"

"But?" She shook her head, thankful he couldn't see her. Eva hated excuses. Everyone knew that. Liam knew that. "It better be a pretty important 'but' because it's a pretty important wedding."

Liam sighed, and started in on how busy he was and how he couldn't just sneak off for a weekend in the mountains whenever he wanted.. Eva tuned Liam's monologue out as she concentrated on the road. The heavy clouds that had been threatening to let go, finally had, and the snow was falling faster and heavier than she would've liked.

"So," she said, interrupting him. "Can you come?"

"Well that's the thing, babe." He paused and the silence was heavy. "I don't think my wife would like it if I skipped out for a whole weekend."

The car swerved and Eva quickly righted it on the road. "Your wife?" she managed to choke out. She'd been expecting bad, but not a wife.

"Yeah, Bridgette. I was going to mention her, but I guess I didn't have the chance yet."

Eva's mind flew through the conversations they'd had.

There hadn't been many, and she did have a tendency to tune him out when he started rambling, but still, she would've remembered a detail like a wife. "You most certainly did not," she said.

"It's no big deal, babe."

"No big deal?" Eva clenched the steering wheel and tried desperately to control her anger so she wouldn't drive herself into the snowy ditch. "I'd say having a wife is a pretty big deal."

"Are you mad?"

"Mad?"

"Yeah, are you mad? Because Bridgette doesn't mind. We have kind of an open—"

"Are you mad?" Eva hollered into the car. "Are you freaking insane, Liam? How can your wife not mind that you're dating me."

"It's not really dating though, is it? I mean, I thought we were just screw—"

"Don't say it," Eva said through clenched teeth. "Do not say one more word."

He was at least smart enough to listen to that piece of advice and silence filled the car, pressing down on Eva until she spoke through clenched teeth, "Don't you have anything to say for yourself?"

"You told me not—"

"Forget it," Eva said, and pushed the button on her cell phone ending the call. "You're not worth it anyway," she said to the empty car.

None of them were. When it came to the men she dated, If it wasn't one thing, it was something else. She probably wouldn't know a decent guy if he walked right up to her and handed her a rose. But a wife? That was a new one. Eva hit the steering wheel with the palm of her hand causing the car to swerve on the ice.

"Dammit," she muttered, and returned her focus to the

road. There was no point dwelling on whatever it had been with Liam, it wasn't serious anyway. But the road conditions were. She clenched her fingers tighter on the wheel and concentrated on making it up the mountain to the Lodge without driving into the ditch. Andi sounded beyond stressed last time they'd spoken and Eva was pretty sure it would put her best friend over the edge if anything happened to delay her arrival.

"You're here!" Andi flew across the foyer and wrapped her arms around Eva before she had a chance to shake the snow off her coat. "What took you so long? I've been expecting you for hours."

Eva wiggled out of her best friend's grasp and took a step back. Andi radiated and her smile was contagious.

"I don't know if you noticed," Eva said with a gesture in the direction of the window. "But there's a blizzard out there."

Andi waved her hand in dismissal. "It's just a few flakes. It's January in the middle of the mountains, what did you expect?"

"Just once, I'd like to come up here in decent weather. Why is it that you're always having some party emergency in the middle of winter?"

Andi shrugged and took Eva's arm in hers. "Come on," she said. "Carmen will have your bags taken up to your room." They walked through the large timber framed lobby, and down a hall that led to the banquet room. "I keep telling you to come and visit in the summertime," Andi said. "If you think it's beautiful with the snow, you should see it with the wildflowers blooming, and the sun sparkling on the pond. It's beyond magical."

Eva stopped short and stared at her friend and business partner that she knew better than anyone. "Are you feeling okay? Because I know it's pretty here and all, but it wasn't that long ago when I never would have heard such crazy things come out of your mouth."

"I know, I know. But ever since—"

"Colin. I know," Eva said good naturedly. "You're in love and that makes the world look brighter. And I'm happy for you." Andi raised an eyebrow and Eva quickly added, "I am." She squeezed Andi's arm. "I really am," she said again, this time looking in her friend's eyes.

After a moment, Andi wrapped her arm around Eva's shoulders and they resumed walking down the hallway toward the banquet room. "I know you are," she said. "And soon you'll know exactly how I'm feeling. I have a good feeling that this new guy. Liam, is it?" Andi glanced up, but without waiting for an answer she kept talking. "I have a feeling that Liam might just be the guy that can handle you and finally make you settle down. Everything you've told me about him, he sounds like—"

"He's an ass."

"Okay," Andi drew the word out and shot Eva a look that she didn't miss. "Should I ask?"

"It's probably better if you don't." Eva shook her head and stepped into the banquet room. "I'm done with men." Eva could feel Andi's eyes watching her as she wandered over to a table and fingered the centrepiece. "We'll have to change these," Eva said. "They're far too Christmasey for a January wedding. If we go with a winter forest theme, they won't be—"

"You're not even going to tell me why?" Andi appeared at her side and took Eva's hand away from the poinsettias. "The centerpieces are fine," she said gently. "Now tell me. What's really going on?"

Eva looked at her friend, and the kindness in her eyes. She missed their girl talk; sitting in the Party Hearty office dishing on the various boys she'd dated and why they would never do. Andi was always a good listener and Eva knew how easy it would be to spill everything. She longed to tell Andi that she was so envious of her loving relationship that it hurt. That she too wanted to settle down and find a man who was more than just a fling. A man who would complement her instead of stifle her, a man who would encourage her independence but make her feel safe and taken care of at the same time. A man, who… it isn't matter. Eva wouldn't say anything. Not with Andi's wedding looming. Besides, things hadn't been the same since Andi met Colin. Her friend was desperately in love with the man who showed her how magical the holidays could be, and fell in love with her in the process. Which was great. It really was, but at the same time, her friend was no longer capable of seeing how truly desperate the dating situation was for the average woman. Well, at least how desperate it was for her.

Eva shook her head and forced a smile she hoped Andi wouldn't see as fake. "There's nothing to talk about. I'm just so overwhelmed with ideas for your big day. And given the fact that you didn't really give me much notice, I don't have time for any distractions." She pulled her oversized portfolio from her tote bag and flipped it open. "See here?"

Eva pointed to a photo of white flowers, pinecones, a dust of what looked like snow, and twigs artfully arranged. The effect, although rustic, was beautiful and absolutely perfect for a wedding at the Lodge. Andi squealed, just the way Eva knew she would. She snatched the portfolio out of Eva's hands and dropped into the chair where she began flipping pages and exclaiming over all the details Eva had thrown together in the past few days.

"You've thought of everything," Andi said when she looked up after a moment. "I can't believe you did this all in only a few days."

Eva shrugged and flipped her long blond hair over her shoulder. "It's not a big deal. After all, it's what I do. What we do," she added pointedly.

"I know, I know," Andi said. "I've been kind of absent

lately, but that will change after the wedding. I promise. It'll be your turn to have a little vacation. You deserve it. Especially with all this."

Eva brushed off the comment. She didn't need to take time off. Besides, Andi and Colin would probably want a honeymoon and she had her work to keep her busy. It's not like she was about to run off to a hot beach with some equally hot guy.

She shifted from foot to foot as she glanced around the room. She was starting to feel the familiar itch to get started with the planning prep. The banquet room was still decorated for the Christmas season that had barely wrapped up. It would take a sold day to strip it down and start getting it dressed for a wedding. And that was only if she had competent people working for her. She was about to ask Andi how many people she'd have from the Lodge staff to help her when Andi grabbed a piece of paper from the portfolio and held it up.

"This is perfect," she exclaimed. "Vows by the pond?"

Eva silently cursed herself. She hadn't been sure her ideas for the ceremony would work out and she didn't want Andi to get excited about something that might not pan out. "Well, as long as it's not too cold or a blizzard or something," Eva said. "Maybe we can have a back up plan, too. We don't want your guests to freeze."

"No," Andi said. She gazed at the photo and said, "It'll be perfect. It's such a small wedding and it's kind of where our first date was."

"I remember. Ice skating," Eva said and added quickly. "Don't worry, I won't make you say 'I do' with skates on."

Andi laughed, but her smile faded quickly and was replaced with immediate tears.

"Andi, are you crying?" Eva knelt so she was face to face with her. "I told you, I'd never make you skate in a wedding dress, I was just—"

"No." Andi waved her hand in a weak attempt to dry her

tears. "It's not that. Sorry, I've just been so emotional lately with everything going on. I swear I'm bursting into tears all the time. It's ridiculous." She wiped her face with a tissue Eva handed her. "Thank you."

"Of course."

"No, I mean for everything. For all of this. I didn't plan on having the ceremony so soon, but when Colin proposed…and then being here again for the holidays, it just felt right, you know?"

Eva nodded even though she most certainly didn't know.

"I just don't want to wait anymore. What's the point, right?"

What was the point indeed, Eva thought. If she had someone who loved her the way Colin loved Andi, she herself might be inclined to break her self assigned rule of never getting married. The idea had tempted her more than once lately, not that she'd admit it to anyone, but there was no point even entertaining the thought when she hadn't met anyone worth the effort in years. Not when all she'd had to choose from were men like Liam.

"I just had an idea." Andi sat up straight. "You'd probably really like Colin's friend, Troy. He's a successful businessman, something to do with paint, I don't know. But I do know he's cute and more importantly, he's single."

"I don't need a date."

"Sure you do," Andi said. "You can't fool me."

Eva froze for a second before grabbing the portfolio away from Andi. She flipped through the pages so she wouldn't have to look up and into her friend's eyes. Andi knew her too well, and the last thing she needed to worry about was Eva's love life. Especially if Andi knew that she'd actually like to have a love life. It was better if everyone, including herself, kept to the original plan of staying single and care free.

"Come on, Andi." Eva forced a lightness into her voice.

"You know me. I don't do serious relationships. I'm more of a casual kind of girl. That's the way I like it." She flinched inwardly at the lie that was becoming hard to keep, especially from herself. "Now, can we get back to work? Do you have any other ideas for the ceremony because we should start nailing down the details."

There was silence for a minute and when Eva allowed herself to look up at Andi's face, she could see the uncertainty there. Thankfully Andi didn't push. Instead she said, "I did have one idea that I think would work really well. Especially if we have the ceremony at the pond."

Eva flipped to a clean page and poised her pen over the page waiting to take note.

"What if I arrived on horse back?" Andi asked.

"Arrived where?"

"The ceremony of course."

"You?" Eva said. "You want to ride a horse in your dress? A stinky barn animal? In a gown? And here I was worried about you on skates."

Andi pushed back from the table and stood, pulling Eva up as well. "It'll be perfect. And seriously romantic. I'm sure there's a white horse in the stables." Andi got that look on her face and Eva knew she was already picturing herself on the horse. "You're going to need to talk to Jeff,"

"Jeff?"

"He's the stable manager. You can work out the details with him."

"Horse details?"

"Yes, silly. Are you feeling okay? You look a little stunned."

Eva shook her head, stunned didn't begin to describe it. "Andi, I don't know. I'm not really the best person to deal with that. I don't do horses."

That was an understatement. Just the thought of a smelly stable was enough to wrinkle her nose, let alone the idea of getting near one of the huge beasts. She'd only been on a horse once and that was enough. She'd been twelve, and at summer camp. Of course that story was far from a happy ending, unless you call a broken arm and a life long distrust of sitting on any four legged creature, a happy ending. Horses were pretty enough to look at, as long as she didn't have to go anywhere near one.

"Please," Andi pleaded. "I know you don't love horses. But I really think it would be great and I just don't have the time to deal with the details. My dad and the boys are arriving in the morning and I need to keep them far away from my mom. I'll have my hands full just with family drama, I really need you."

"What about your dad's wife?"

"Roxanne?" Andi rolled her eyes and quickly added a sweet smile. "Oh, she'll be coming later. She said she couldn't bear to be in the mountains one day longer than she needed to be."

Eva gave her a conspiratorial grin and as they both knew she would, she nodded. "I'll take care of it," Eva said. Of course she'd do it. But it didn't matter what Andi said, best friend or not, she wasn't getting anywhere near an actual horse.

If Eva's struggling with the idea of a horse now, wait until she meets Jeff, the ranch hand at the Lodge! Sparks are certain to fly when she meets the handsome cowboy! Read the rest of Mistaken Gifts NOW!

About the Author

Elena Aitken is a USA Today Bestselling Author of more than forty romance and women's fiction novels. The mother of 'grown up' twins, Elena now lives with her very own mountain man in the heart of the very mountains she writes about. She can often be found with her toes in the lake and a glass of wine in her hand, dreaming up her next book and working on her own happily ever after.

To learn more about Elena:
www.elenaaitken.com
elena@elenaaitken.com